MW00884006

Book 2, New Vampire Disorder

By Marie Johnston

Rourke

Editing by The Killion Group Inc.

Cover by P and N Graphics

Rourke
Book Two, New Vampire Disorder

Grace Otto was a vampire child adopted by humans and raised in a secluded but loving environment. When she stumbles across their murders, she comes face to face with Rourke, the male who's haunted her nightmares, who might have killed her birth family. It's not long before she realizes the mysterious male is not the one responsible for her parents' demise, but their pasts are irrevocably linked and she's forced to leave the human world to find out how.

Around Grace, Rourke dares to think of a better future, one that can overwrite his traumatic history. Until she unwittingly commits an act of betrayal that threatens her and their entire species. To save Grace, Rourke will need to hunt down the demons of their past.

To all the readers who love brooding vampires as much as I do.

Chapter One

They aren't moving. No need to ask why. Even her young mind comprehended the violence she'd heard while she squeezed her eyes shut. Eerie stillness surrounded her as she opened her eyes to a tall, dark male stalking through the pools of her parents' blood. His black eyes searched the room, but she lay hidden under the settee where she'd crawled once the screaming started. The shine of streetlamps reflected off his ebony hair every time he passed a window and shadowed the harsh planes of his face, making him look like the killer he was.

Her sensitive ears picked up rapid footsteps outside. The breath froze in her lungs as his gaze swept over her hiding spot. Tears that had been imprisoned behind her eyelids rolled down her cheeks. He glanced at the front door, then back to the settee. With a nod, he strode out of the room and disappeared.

A bell chimed.

Grace Otto frowned. A doorbell? That had never been a part of her recurring dream before.

Another chime roused her fully from sleep. Her eyes fluttered open. She heard the sound again and rolled over to answer her phone.

"Hey, kiddo," her dad greeted. "If you're up for the night, why don't you hit the Bullhead Trail with us?"

She thought about his offer for all of three seconds. Record an online lesson she could do anytime or go hiking with her family who were the most awesome people *ever*? "See you in forty-five."

A half hour later, she was dressed in her favorite Freemont-U sweater, a durable pair of jeans and her trail shoes. Her deep henna-colored hair was pulled back into a ponytail. She was the oddity in her family—a vampire. It didn't diminish their love for her, the little two-year-old they'd rescued.

Her mom, dad, and brother had all gone out to eat, leaving her home. The invite had extended to her, of course, but she had been up until well into midmorning working her at-home tutoring job. She hopped into her maroon Rav4 and drove straight to the Bullhead that wound along the river separating Freemont from its ugly step-sister West Creek.

The lot at the trailhead where she was to meet her family sat empty. Perhaps they went... Where would they go at ten at night? Grace parked and stepped out. A thick cloud of blood hung in the air. Grace knew the smell. Knew it like her next breath.

"Mom? Dad?" Panic rose as she searched the darkness. "Nathaniel?"

She rarely fed from Nathaniel, but of course she recognized her older brother's scent lingering in the night along with her parents'. Why would their blood taint the air?

Funny how some memories rush back as soon as a trigger hits the brain. She was barely a toddler when her birth family had been slaughtered. She didn't remember much, just what her terrifying dreams showed her. But every drop of blood she scented flashed a slide show of gruesome images through her mind.

She took off running, knowing all the trails well, and charged into where the blood fog was thickest.

No, no, no. Could she find them alive and well when the aroma clogged her senses so significantly?

The stench of shifter and sulfur hit her. She slowed and went into hiding mode, stepping off the trail into the trees. Their leaves offered little concealment during the fall, but it was all she had.

Voices.

"We need you to come out and look at this." A male voice spoke with urgency. Grace inhaled deeply. He was a shifter and not the origin of the sulfur stench. She didn't feel any menace radiating off the males. The way they walked and the way they dressed, she thought of a police SWAT team, only supernatural.

"Vampires attacked a human family," he continued. "but there's something I think is your specialty. There's a mile marker on the county road.

If you've driven down this way before, you can just flash here."

Attacked a human family? No…it couldn't be. Her dad had *just* called her…nearly an hour ago… She inched closer, worried they'd hear her chaotic heartbeat, until movement stopped her. Two others had arrived, vampires and both male. As they neared, she peered through the night to get a better look. Her jaw dropped and her lungs stalled.

It was *him*. Her nightmare male was supposed to be imaginary. A figure that haunted her sleep, fabricated in the brain of a child. In real life, he was more imposing.

He carefully stepped over a large object covered by the undergrowth.

She squinted, trying to get clearer picture. A gasp caught in her throat, her mouth dropped open in a silent scream.

He had avoided her mother's bloody, ravaged body.

This couldn't be happening again. Death. Him. Being helpless.

Her mother's throat was ripped out. Grace choked back a sob. The male's head cocked, his eyes narrowed to scan the woods. She bit her lip, but not enough to draw blood, and held her breath. Another vampire, a large blond goliath, walked to stand next to the first male. They wore the same grim expression.

The shifter she'd heard on the phone approached the dark male. *Her* male.

"The crime scene is all yours. We didn't touch anything, not after what we smelled." The shifter trotted to the road where a charcoal SUV idled. Within seconds, he was gone, leaving her alone with the two males and her family's remains.

From her spot in the bushes, Grace tracked the vampire's movements even though he was a hundred yards away. Only her loathing of the male, the one who embodied her nightmares, played the starring role in most of them, dammed her grief as he walked among the remains of her family.

Had killing her birth family not been enough?

His attention was drawn back to the body of her father, where it had landed after being flung by an unknown force, his throat ripped out. Grace blinked rapidly to keep her tears at bay.

Oh god, her brother. The blond giant was looking up, and when she followed his gaze, she realized he studied Nathaniel's body. His remains were strung over a heavy branch of one of the park's cottonwoods and a tiny rivulet of blood dribbled through the bark. A tear from each eye spilled over to run down her cheeks. She shook with the effort of holding back a cry of anguish.

The tall male she detested murmured something to the goliath. Both males' demeanors were serious. Grace grudgingly admitted they appeared to take no joy in her family's demise. They seemed as confounded as she.

Together, the two inspected her dad. Her nightmare male retrieved a phone out of the pocket of his black leather pants and snapped a few pictures. When he moved to inspect her mother, the blond circled the tree. Grace flinched when he suddenly jumped up to a large branch, and just as quickly her nightmare male's gaze jerked up.

She froze. Had he heard her, or did he think it was just the big male?

Nightmare male stood frowning at the blond in the tree who was now taking pictures of her brother. His obsidian gaze finally returned to the body in front of him. As if satisfied, he stalked to the base of the tree cradling Nathaniel's body.

To Grace's amazement, the blond carefully and respectfully lowered her brother's body. Nightmare male caught him and quickly laid him next to their mother. Then both males hauled her dad to the line-up.

"The Guardian told you where the car was stashed." A voice like caramel washed over her, but was lost in her anguish.

Her adopted dad had always told her vampires killed her birth parents. Regardless of her being a vampire, they'd raised her with love and acceptance, coloring her view of the world as being better than it was. She would not be fooled by this guy. He could be the most handsome male she'd ever seen, but she knew the black heart that beat in his broad, muscular chest.

The big one walked to the road and when he reached it, hung a left. She wished she could follow, but they'd hear her.

A whoosh of wind ruffled some loose strands of hair. She lifted her gaze off the goliath to find herself looking into a pair of jet-black eyes. As she gasped, she registered that she was wrong. His irises were not entirely black, and the dark brown mirrored her stunned expression.

His gaze was cold, calculating, and directed at her.

Eyes wide, heart pounding, she flashed away.

Appearing next to her vehicle, she dug into her pockets for her keys—and dropped them.

She stooped to grab them, but a brush of air caressed her bare neck. She shot up straight, prepared to fight.

His reflection stared back at her from her car window, moonlight gleaming off his ebony hair. His head tilted imperceptibly as his eyes focused on her.

Grace sucked in a breath. She couldn't scream—it was futile. He was so close his heat radiated into her. If she wasn't terrified of him, it'd snake into her and settle in deep on this cool night.

Summoning all her strength, she shoved an elbow back into his gut. He easily deflected, and, oh shit, she was in trouble. She didn't know how to fight. He'd been around three dead bodies and was stalking her without even an increase in heart rhythm.

She flashed again, this time a mile up Bullhead.

Her breath puffed in the autumn air, her breathing ragged. She blanched when he formed in front of her. His scent, free from the cloud of death and despair, surrounded her. He smelled…edible. Hickory chips smoking in the grill delicious. Her opinion was not on par with her body's reaction to his scent.

"Why were you spying on us?" He stood with his arms crossed as if patiently waiting for her answer.

Involuntarily, she shivered. *That voice!* His smell! Coupled with his looks—he was dangerous on many levels.

She flashed again, two more miles up the trail. Her logical mind informed her that he'd followed her twice already. She hadn't even known it was possible.

He appeared in front of her, an eyebrow arched. "Did you have something to do with the humans' deaths?"

At the mention of her parents, she went wild.

For all the good it did.

She punched, she kicked, she kneed. All easily deflected. He clasped her arms to pull her toward him and spin her around. Both of her legs pumped and flailed, trying to kick back into his shins or loosen his grip, but he restrained her like it was something he did every day.

From his domineering presence and grim demeanor, maybe he did.

He jolted her so hard her teeth clattered. It stunned her into momentary stillness. When she tensed to start all over again, he repeated the movement—harder. Her breath whooshed out.

She struggled to inhale against his vice-like grip. He was an immobile wall at her back. Humiliatingly enough, she wanted to seek comfort in that wall.

Tears pricked her eyes. She sniffled.

His grip loosened, then tightened again. "Don't think that'll work on me," he sneered into her ear.

The dam broke and sob after sob escaped her.

***

Rourke didn't know what to do.

The beautiful suspect's tears were real. Not, *oh I'm female and I'll make you do what I want by crying* nor *I can't tell the pleasure from the pain, Rourke. Release the cuffs.* He heard the latter all the time. In fact, he strove for it.

But this female cried for real. Her heart was broken. Had she known that family, been close to them?

Her curly hair tickled his nose as her short ponytail bobbed with her sobs. Her presence at the crime scene became clear to him shortly after he'd arrived. Through the din of death, sulfur, and the shifters who'd called them in, her scent had curled around him. Lemonade after a hot night's work.

He fucking hated lemonade.

Or he used to. Now he wanted a taste of her. Would she be sharp but sweet?

His blood supply moved in a southward direction, but he cut off that line of thinking. Arousal did not happen unless he commanded it.

Unfortunately, his pestering cock didn't get the message.

Tilting his pelvis back to not press into her, he discovered her shorter stature still allowed her to curve back into him.

His damn arms didn't seem to want to let her go. He forced his grip to loosen, and she slid down his body to collapse on the ground.

His eyelids drifted shut at the sensation, but he snapped them open. Her legs were curled under her, her face buried in her hands while she continued to weep.

Loss and sorrow pulsed from her.

"You knew them." He stated the obvious, but needed to say something.

She nodded and inhaled a shuddering breath attempting to regain her composure. He silently cheered her on, selfishly wanting to see her gingerbread brown eyes again.

"Who were they to you?" he asked

Her shoulders slumped, bringing his attention to her body. It was unlike him. In the field, he assessed everyone and everything with cold calculation. In his decrepit excuse for a personal life, he selected females based on their athletic frame. His bedroom activities required the stamina. He almost slept solely with vampires for that reason.

While this little dove was a vampire, she sported the most uncommon curves found in their kind. He estimated her to be about five-six—damn near petite in the vampire world.

She spoke, shaking him out of his inappropriate perusal. "They were my family."

He rocked back in disbelief. "*Humans?*"

She made a disgusted sound he assumed was aimed at his reaction. "They adopted me after my birth family was—" she peeked over shoulder, eyes narrowed untrustingly on him, "killed."

Spoken as if it was his fault?

He couldn't hide his incredulity. "Humans *adopted* you. Did they know you were a vampire?"

"Not every species are soulless murderers," she murmured.

"Insinuating vampires were responsible for your first family's deaths."

"You should know."

His standard coolness returned. She had no idea. "Do you know who killed your family tonight?"

She wiped her face off on her sweater. It was the worst thing that could've happened to him. The bottom hem lifted to reveal a creamy swatch of bronzed skin.

His blood supply plummeted straight to his groin. Inconvenient.

"I don't know. I was supposed to meet them to go hiking tonight. When I got to our meeting place, I smelled…" a frustrated noise escaped her, suggesting she was trying not to break down again and was pissed it wasn't working, "…death, their blood."

He stared down at the living conundrum. A vampire adopted by humans. A petite vampire. He doubted she was also a suspect, but she might help them figure out what was going on.

His phone vibrated. Rourke palmed it out of his pocket.

Got her?

He texted back, Yes. Clean up?

Got it.

Meaning Bishop had grabbed the car and would load up the bodies and dispose of them. They needed to protect the existence of their kind, even if it meant making a human family appear as if they went missing.

The young vampire at his feet wouldn't approve.

"What's your name?" he asked. The urge to crouch down and soothe her somehow struck him and…it was…odd.

Nurturing, comforting, soothing and whatever else *Thesaurus.com* churned out did not describe him. He'd never had the interest. Some millionaire shrink with a TV show might suggest severe abuse as a child had hardened him against hurt.

"Grace."

A beautiful, serene name for a crumpled, distraught female out in the woods.

"Grace," he repeated. The word slowly burned into his conscious.

Maybe he should switch with Bishop.

No. He shouldn't. A surge of rage tore through him at the idea of another male alone with her. Grace peered up at him sensing his anger, a hint of fear in her eyes.

The next emotion was regret, shame that he was the reason for it.

Hellfire. These *feelings* going through him rivaled a human in the throes of puberty. He didn't *feel*, period.

"Are you responsible for killing my family?" The accusation in her tone—she'd already assumed the answer.

The question struck him as absurd. "I gave up massacring humans decades ago." A sharp twang of hatred lifted from her. Did she think he was serious? "Relax, angel. Killing defenseless creatures has never been my style, though humans wouldn't show the same reserve for us."

She wasn't appeased.

He didn't care.

He *shouldn't* care.

But it bothered him. And it bothered him that it bothered him.

He didn't feel.

"I'm going to find out who did, and I'm going to rip them apart worse than they did my family." Resolute. No boasting.

He'd believe her—if he could allow that to happen. "My team and I will investigate this, it's what we do. We'll start with you coming back to our headquarters."

She jumped up faster than he could blink. *No one* startled him like that. He'd need to meditate for hours to straighten the upheaval this girl caused within him.

"*I'm* going down to the crime scene. I don't want you near them." Her eyes glittered with defiance, her gaze caught on his holstered gun.

He read her intentions. "Don't even think about it." His voice was quiet, hard.

She sucked in a breath and met his steady gaze. "Or what?"

Her fear washed over him, and…it bothered him. "Or I'll detain you before your fingers touch metal and throw you into a holding cell."

A blink of confusion flashed through her expression. "Holding cell?"

Rourke barked out a laugh. "What'd you think I'd do?" His laughter died. The answer was written across her pale face. "I wouldn't have faulted you for defending yourself, just been annoyed. But I need to take you somewhere so you can tell us what you know, and I can get back to investigating these murders."

She studied him for a heartbeat before shaking her head. "No. I need to go there, too, and look around."

A bad idea if he'd ever heard one. "Angel, we've been at this a long time. What do you think you'll find that we can't?"

She glared at him with those eyes that tempted him to step into a different world, one where violence wasn't a steady diet in his life. "What's your name?"

Not the statement he'd been expecting. "Rourke."

"Let me explain." Her voice dripped sappy sweet, like she had to talk slow so he could keep up. "I was raised with them. I know their smells, their habits. I know who their friends and acquaintances are, and more importantly, I know *their* smells, too. If any one of them had anything to do with tonight, I'll know. Tell me, *Rourke*, what can you do down there?"

Learn whether or not demons had been involved, but that wasn't a detail he'd be sharing with her. She was right about knowing the smells, however. If she could stomach wading through the details, she might have unique insight.

"What would you do if it was your family?" she challenged.

One question and the unusual spikes of good mood vanished. He was ice. "I'd track down the bastards who did it and thank them."

She tilted her head. The faint light of the moon danced through her hair. "I'm not surprised."

The arch tone in her voice irritated him. He wrapped his hand around her upper arm and flashed her back to the murder ground.

"What the hell, dude?" She yanked her arm away and stumbled a few steps back.

Bishop shut the trunk of the human's car and threw a questioning look Rourke's way.

"She wants to help," Rourke answered, irritation heavy in his voice. "Grace, this is my partner Bishop."

"What are you doing with their car?" Grace scanned the area, the one that no longer held three bodies. "Are my mom, dad, and brother in there? What are you going to do with it, make it look like an accident?"

Way more gruesome and thorough than that, angel.

His buddy was shit at hiding what he was thinking, and Grace picked up on that right away. Shocked disbelief radiated off of her.

She spun on him. "What is he doing with them?"

"I'll tell you, but never forget one thing. Rule number one is to protect our species." When she grudgingly nodded, he continued, "We have a contact in the junk yard. He'll crush the car with the bodies inside and drop it in the bed of one of our trucks. Then we'll bury it where no human will ever find them."

Her face turned ashen; her distain surrounded Rourke. Bishop dropped his head and cursed.

"Why?" Her rage made her voice quiver.

"Remember rule number one? Protect our people. We'll clean out their house, and if you live with them, your life with it. Eventually the bank will get it, people will wonder what happened, but then they'll forget. Meaning, they won't look for them—or you—and therefore, they won't find out they're dead, and vampires were involved. You can't go home."

The smack across his face echoed through the clearing. The fury behind her hit added more force than he'd have guessed. The eyes of Bishop rivaled the size of the moon.

For an eighty-four-year-old vampire, this young thing was really catching him unaware.

He worked his jaw. Plenty of females *slapped* him. Grace hit him with an open-hand. There was a difference.

"I wouldn't do that again." His warning should've made her quake in her sensible hiking shoes.

"Or what? You'll bury my family in some cold, dark grave where everyone can forget about them? You'll move me out of my home—*without my permission?* Tell me, Rourke, what else will you do?"

"Lock you up and leave you out of this investigation entirely."

Grace clamped her mouth shut, her full lower lip sticking out slightly, mesmerizing him.

He waited for her decision. On this, he would not compromise.

She glanced back over her shoulder where Bishop stood rigidly, watching the play between them. Her watery eyes lingered on the car, white teeth nibbled on her lower lip. She struggled to maintain her composure.

"Do they have to be crushed, too? Can't we bury them deep in the hills?"

"We don't have the manpower." Not with the underworld causing problems that could affect all the races roaming the planet.

"My dead family has obviously never bothered you, but I will not let you crush them in a heap of metal like they're trash that needs to be hidden." Vibrations ran through her muscles, rose red bled into her eyes. She disappeared.

He spun toward the car where she reappeared. Surprise filled Bishop's expression as he angled toward her. She ripped the car door open and dove inside. Bishop reached for her, but Rourke beat him to the door. She locked it.

He couldn't ruin the car. They still had to drive it to the junk yard and couldn't draw attention. He flashed to the passenger side and opened the door. "Grace, listen to me."

She screamed and clambered to open the door, but it was still locked.

With a sigh, he slid into the passenger seat. She kicked at him, but he caught her legs and pulled her toward him. She yelped as she bounced over the console. He dropped her legs and caught her shoulders.

"All right," he snapped.

Her struggles weakened.

"We'll bury them, okay?"

The fear in her eyes morphed into trepidation that he lied. "Why would you do that?"

He wanted to fucking know, too. "Because you went ballistic. I'll dig the damn hole myself."

"I'll take care of it," Bishop offered from outside the car. He shrugged at Rourke's furious expression. "She's killing me. I didn't know they were her people."

Rourke released her and she scrambled out of the car to face Bishop.

"Thank you."

Her grateful smile did two things to Rourke: anger him it wasn't aimed toward him and introduce shame back into his emotional repertoire. Twice tonight, must be a record.

"I have to say goodbye." Hastily wiping her eyes, she trudged back toward the car. Bishop shuffled to the side, glancing at the vehicle like he was reorganizing how he would've arranged the bodies for her viewing.

Rourke folded his arms across his chest and glowered at her, then at Bishop, who opened the trunk with this fob before folding his hands respectfully in front of him, head bowed.

As for Rourke, he didn't let her out of his sight.

Her shoulders drooped, her head dropped. He smelled her tears as she silently wept. She reached in to stroke her brother's ravaged face. He had also worn a Freemont-U sweater now dried into a rusty brown color from his blood. Her parents had dressed for the outdoors, no indication they were up to anything nefarious other than a nighttime hike with their vampire daughter.

She moved around to the door and bent inside, her body shaking.

Logically, he knew there were warm, loving families out there, even in the vampire world. What must it be like to be a part of one? He followed a male who'd come from a family whose dynamics were similar to Grace's. It had molded Demetrius into a male Rourke had decided to follow to the death as soon as he'd met him.

After they'd brawled in an alley until neither of them could stand.

Grace shut the trunk door, staying her hand for a heartbeat on the frame. "Why is there the faint smell of a book of matches?"

He and Bishop exchanged looks. Rourke calculated the risks of telling her what their society faced. If she happened to be cooperating with demons, she'd know about them anyway. His intuition told him she wasn't, but he didn't trust easily. He trusted his inner circle and that was it. If she didn't know about demons, perhaps her assistance into the case would be beneficial.

"Brimstone."

"I know the sulfur smell, but where's it from?"

"Where else?"

She blinked and stepped away from the car. "Brimstone for real? Are you saying the smell came from Hell?"

"Bingo."

Before they could continue their conversation, Bishop went around the car to get inside. "I need to get going to finish everything before daybreak."

Grace awarded him a soft smile of thanks. For two seconds, Rourke hated the guy.

"What does that mean?" She roamed the area, smelling and inspecting every tree, each blade of grass. She stepped nimbly through the pile of leaves dumped from the branches.

"Demons are trying to infiltrate themselves into our race, aiming to open a portal that will allow the Circle of Thirteen free access to our realm."

Grace stopped to stare at him. "Seriously?"

He inclined his head once. Usually accused of being *too* serious, he wasn't sure if she was legitimately asking.

"And this circle—demons?"

"All thirteen of them. There's more of course, these are the most powerful. Rulers of the underworld, if you will. Possession is the key, but finding thirteen powerful hosts to take over has proven challenging for them. Not many vampires buy their whole my-power-is-your-power spiel."

Squatting down, she shuffled through a pile of dried, brown leaves. "Why vampires and not shifters or humans?"

"Don't you know, angel? We're inherently more evil than shifters? That's why we walk in the dark, and all that bullshit, while shifters frolic in the woods."

Chapter Two

The only reason Grace wasn't wallowing in her grief was because of her determination to follow this through. She needed to *do* something—for her family. Even it meant cooperating with Rourke, who she should hate and fear.

Yet…he'd done nothing to earn those feelings. He'd even been almost compassionate. A man who indiscriminately murders parents of small children doesn't help victims investigate their loved ones' murders, or offer to bury them because it destroyed her to think of them crushed.

Unless he was playing her for some reason. What would it be? He didn't portray a male who'd invest himself in a scheme. He followed thought by action, not manipulation.

"Is it because we drink blood that we're supposed to be evil?" She crept along the ground, using all her senses to ferret out a clue.

"Which came first the chicken or the egg? Did we turn evil because we drank blood, or did we drink blood because we were evil?" Rourke followed her. She wanted to scream at him to help her, but he seemed more intent on monitoring her progress. "Although many shifters I've met over the last several decades liked their meat pretty damn raw."

"Decades?" she echoed, glancing up at him. The male looked about thirty, tops.

His eyes narrowed on her. "Decades, angel. You knew that part right?"

Defensiveness returned to her spine. "My parents taught me a lot." *I just haven't met any other vampires.*

His dark gaze, unnerving in its intensity, remained pinned on her. "Why, when you say certain things, do I feel like you're blaming me for the all the wrongs in the world?"

Because she did. Couldn't prove it, but he was involved in her families' deaths somehow. Her dream told her. And it was true. Right? "If that's the way you're interpreting my words, it's not my problem."

His midnight gaze scrutinized her.

She rose and continued her search in an effort to divert his unnerving attention, and her wavering conviction in his role in her nightmare. "What's your take on what happened?

"Ladies first." He hadn't moved. Crossing his arms, biceps flexing, he waited.

"I didn't go to school for forensics." Facing him, she put her hands on her hips.

He rolled a shoulder. "Give it a shot."

Pointing to the road, she laid out her assumption of how events played out. "The shifters said they moved their car and got their— " she gulped, she could do this, "—bodies off the road. Someone stopped my parents and attacked. The killers waited, somehow knowing they'd be out here." Letting her hand fall, she returned her attention back to him. "And demons were involved. That's all I got."

He inclined his head, moonlight glinting off his raven hair, giving him an otherworld appeal. As if he needed more appeal. "It's possible it was a murder of convenience. If the murderers hunted here enough, humans were bound to show up for a night hike."

Grace's shoulders drooped. As if she didn't feel guilty enough, her family would be alive if they hadn't accommodated her paranormal needs. Finding out who was responsible pushed aside those feelings. They'd accomplish nothing. She nimbly stepped through the trees, all her senses working at full capacity.

Rourke studied her. The burn of his assessing gaze on her body making her curse her heightened senses, and him. Why couldn't it have been the goliath who stayed behind? He at least seemed to have more empathy than a brick.

"I'm going to check the other side of the road." She was relieved to increase the distance between them, only to feel a trickle between her shoulder blades.

Glancing over her shoulder, she jumped. Rourke had followed her, now not three feet behind. That damn eyebrow cocked again. She ignored him and hurried across the road.

Nothing. Not one drop of blood and the scent of brimstone dropped drastically.

"The action was all on the other side where we were." She brushed a stray strand of hair off her face.

His eyes followed her actions, his expression unreadable. "It appears so."

He didn't elaborate. With a disgusted sigh, she stomped across the road. No tire marks. Her dad had stopped intentionally. Thinking someone needed help? Then her dad, mom, and brother had all been slaughtered. The pale faces, caught in the grimace of death, rose in her mind. Grace's throat swelled. She blinked rapidly to keep the tears at bay.

She rerouted her mind to the task at hand. "Their blood was consumed."

A glint of approval entered his black gaze. "Much of it, yes."

Her eyes widened. "That's why you're not helping? You've already read the crime scene and you're just humoring me?"

"You wanted to help."

"Of course I did. My family was slaughtered." Tears pricked behind her eyes. She *would not cry* in front of him again. "Do you have any idea what that feels like?"

His handsome features clouded over. "It was very freeing to not have to do it myself."

He hadn't been joking before about thanking his family's murderers?

"Your relatives are even worse than you?" Her retort slipped out before she could sensor herself. Dammit, why didn't she think before spewing the first thing that popped to mind?

"You have no idea, angel."

His intensity increased tenfold, like a blinding light. She averted her eyes.

A small silver speck captured her attention. Something lay by the base of a tree.

"What is that?" She crept closer. "Maybe that's where they waited for their victims to drive by."

A glance at Rourke stopped her in her tracks. His brow was furrowed with interest. The first she'd seen all night.

"What?" he asked, bypassing her to reach the spot first.

He knelt and uncovered the silver object. Grace waited for him to pick it up, but he stared at it so long, she bent to do it herself. He snatched it up and pocketed it.

"Whoa. What the hell? Lemme see it."

He rose and gripped her elbow and the world blinked away. When she reoriented, she faced a large, square gray building with limited windows in front of her.

She peered up at the concrete monstrosity. "Where are we?"

"Headquarters."

He hauled her toward a door.

"And? What was the thing you found?"

He pulled her through the door that opened into a barren hallway. "Just something left behind, probably by a hiker. I doubt it has anything to do with the murders."

"Bullshit." When he flicked a hard look her way, she continued. "I can smell your lie, and it's *my family's* murder. We agreed I'd help, and I want to see what I found."

Her words fell on uncaring ears.

Grace dug in her heels and yanked her arm back. His hand snapped off and he skidded to a halt. She'd have the bruises to prove the force of his hold on her.

She was treated to another expression in his arsenal. Shock. He wasn't a male who was taken by surprise often. She grinned in triumph.

"Show me." Motioning with her fingers, she also tapped her foot to show she meant business.

Back to stone cold Rourke, he dug out the slender metal object.

She plucked it away from him. While examining the object that resembled one half of tweezers, she absentmindedly rubbed her sore elbow.

"Did I hurt you?" Rourke was racking up all kinds of expressions and this one was a twofer—confusion mixed with dismay.

~32~

"Yeah, but it's already healing. Just aches a bit." She held the item up to the exterior light mounted above them. "What do you think it is? Rourke?"

His troubled gaze hadn't left her arm.

Driven to ease his worry, she said, "It's not like you meant to."

"That's just it. I didn't mean to," he mumbled before spinning away.

Whatever that meant. She rushed behind his tall form, noting how his tapered waist transformed into a powerful stride she struggled to keep up with.

How could she feel like this? He'd had her in his grip, his strength obvious. Her reaction? Irritation he'd taken the trinket. Nowhere near the fear her dream gave her. It was like Rourke and her dream male were two different vampires.

"It's a pick from a lock pick kit." He lifted his palm, a silent demand for her to give him back their find.

When she didn't, he glowered at her.

He didn't break stride and neither did she, though she took two steps for his every one. "Say the magic word."

Your ornery nature will get you into trouble. Her dad's words floated through her mind. *Make it a strength, not a weakness.*

Wonder what her dad would consider it now, poking the beast like she was.

Rourke's hand snapped shut and dropped to his side. She fought a grin over her completely inconsequential victory.

"Do you think it's a clue?"

A muscle in his jaw flexed. "No."

"Bullshit."

It happened so quick, but the corner of his mouth twitched. "Is that your favorite word?"

"When I'm being lied to, yes."

"What makes you think I lie?"

"Duh, I can sense it."

There it was again. Confusion mixed with dismay.

"Do others not sense it so easily?" she asked.

"No." The finality of his tone said that was all she was going to get.

He abruptly turned into an office. Grace had to backtrack to follow him in.

An older female sat at a desk inside. Her scent was vampire and by the looks of her she must be centuries old. Her serene presence and the wisdom in her eyes, with her white hair and patterned dress to her ankles, instantly comforted Grace. If she could to pick someone to cradle her while she cried for days, this female topped the list.

Grace ached to close herself into a dark room and let loose the pain and loss balled tightly inside of her.

"Betty." The warmth in Rourke's voice startled Grace. "Has Demetrius returned?"

Grace pulled her attention from her coiled emotion to assess her situation. Swanky office, Rourke's deferent tone, and Betty the assistant. Demetrius must be the big vampire on campus.

"He and Lady Callista are still briefing the TriSpecies Synod. I expect them back soon." Betty's mouth quirked, and she shot Rourke a knowing look. "But Master doesn't always tell me right away, not when he's with his young bride."

Rourke cleared his throat as if he was a chaste male and the talk of sex disconcerted him.

Betty paused, glancing back and forth between him and Grace. "I shall summon you when he arrives. Perhaps I can ready a room for our guest?"

"You're not a housekeeper any longer, Betty. I'll leave him a message. Grace is assisting with a case. I'll arrange her lodging."

"I see." Betty's gaze darted between them. She dipped her head toward Grace. "Please, let me know if you need anything."

Rourke thanked her and ushered Grace out of the office.

"She was sweet," Grace whispered. An old vampire like Betty would either have stellar hearing or hardly any.

"She's something." He refused to meet her gaze.

"I love her mix of old world manners and highly inappropriate comments."

"Blame the premium cable Demetrius splurged on for the place. Betty's addicted."

Grace smiled, albeit a sad one. She hiccupped back a sob, determined to hold her personal anguish in. He flinched at the sound, but he remained silent for the long trek to a plain door. He punched rapidly into a key pad and the door slid open.

In front of Grace lay the most utilitarian environment she'd ever seen. Used to throw pillows, vibrant colors, and a homey feel, the space greeting her was cold, gray, and barren. A stainless steel kitchen with bare counters sat across from the door. One couch rested at the edge of the main area while the dining room was devoid of any furniture.

She wandered in. "Do you keep an empty apartment for guests?"

"This is where I live."

Her eyebrows shot up. Perhaps the room paralleled him, with hidden depth. Then it dawned on her. "I'm staying here with you?"

"I can't let you roam freely." His tone was devoid of emotion. By now, she suspected he did it purposely.

Her mouth worked, but no words came out. Sleep? In his place? While he was there?

He was the reason for her sleepless days, but her instincts screamed he wasn't the enemy. Her recurrent nightmares featuring Rourke weren't a coincidence. She'd resolved to get close, find out the truth behind both of her families' death. Was the depth of her sorrow lessening the fear she should have of Rourke? Was it because with no mother or father to spend her evenings with, and with no

Nathaniel to confide in, her social circle was now comprised of a goliath who'd showed her an ounce of kindness, a lovely elderly female, and a male she shouldn't trust?

Blinking rapidly, she tried to recall all the reasons she swore not to break down around him—again.

Oh damn. Bring on the water works. She frantically searched for privacy.

Hellfire. She was crying again.

He barely made out her asking where the bathroom was.

"Down the hall to the left."

She scurried away, looking adorable in her sweatshirt and denim. He'd never had a female in his suite. Not even the females on his team, Zoey and Ophelia. Betty stuck to her suite or her office, and the only other females around were Demetrius's mate and his sister who never left her room.

He wasn't sure how he felt about Grace being here. He didn't *feel*, there should be nothing to question. Regardless, she couldn't go to her house. They still needed to search it. More than a little animosity oozed from her toward him when he sensed none toward Bishop or Betty. It was an unfair comparison. They were the two most likable vampires in the building. Or that he knew, period.

Grace's sobs echoed from the bathroom. She'd sought privacy. He wouldn't bother her, even if she still held the lock pick she'd found at the site.

Allowing her to assist had turned out be an advantage. He'd missed it in his search, so had the Guardians and Bishop. The bodies and scents lingering at the scene had stolen their focus.

His eyes landed on the bathroom door. What must it be like to mourn a family? To have cared about them enough to feel sad when something bad befell them. If he could hunt the rest of his kin down and terminate them, he would. To do so would be to confess everything they'd put him through, and that was his own private hell. His parents' existence was no more. His brother had slunk back to the dank sewers they'd originated from, and Rourke had fallen in with a worthy male. The way Demetrius championed the innocent called to Rourke deeply.

Except when one of the innocent was sobbing in his apartment. He scowled when he realized his front door hung open. Grace intruded on all of his best judgement. Take now, when ideas of knocking on the door and asking if she was okay invaded his mind. He didn't do that shit. After he unhooked his sexual partners—their bodies covered in delicious red marks, quivering from pain so defined their nerves had confused it with pleasure—he walked away. Clean up was their issue.

Grace wasn't his sexual partner. He groaned. A force akin to being kneed in the sac ricocheted through his body at the thought of her not being his. He was an eighty-four-year-old male. Why the hell did it seem like puberty was sneaking up on him again? What next? Was his voice going to crack?

Silently, he walked past the bathroom. Water splashed. He heard her rummaging around for a washcloth. He'd just met her but knew it'd only take minutes before she composed herself and strode out like she owned the place.

In his bedroom, he didn't bother switching on the light. Digging through a cabinet, he located his stash of lock picking mechanisms. Some vampires knitted, at least Betty did, but his hobby was making sure he could get out of any restraints he might find himself in again.

When a family sells their boy as a blood slave, it leaves a guy with need to know he can escape anything. He combined his lock picking talent with sex by restraining his partners and releasing them without using a key—after he was done with them. He got practice and sexual release, both without being bound himself. His partners never complained.

However, one of his partners had stolen from him. Rourke opened one lock pick kit, saw all the pieces were present, dropped it and chose another. In the third kit, one piece was missing. Grace held it in her pocket.

He'd known it was his as soon as he laid eyes on it. He brought the kit to his nose, inhaling deeply, letting his memories sort through the last time he'd used it and with whom. An answer sprang to mind.

Grace exited the bathroom, her soft pads heading back out to the main area. Rourke dropped the kit and closed the drawer, following her out.

She was looking around, searching for him. He could see her brain work as she studied his stark living environment.

"I'm not much of a decorator, I'm afraid."

She jumped and spun around, her hand on her heart. "Good god, Rourke. Give a girl warning."

Again, he marveled at her ability to recover her composure. Quite an ability for a girl raised by humans, but then, a family who adopted a vampire baby wasn't ordinary. Rourke planned to discover how they'd been in the right place at the right time to save Grace.

"You can take the couch for the night." He frowned.

She'd curl up on his couch while he tucked into his pillow-top king-sized mattress, the one luxury he granted himself after years of sleeping on a frigid dirt floor. Her on the couch, him in his bed. Wrong on more than one level. He'd offer his bed, but he couldn't. Just, no. Her in bed *with* him, maybe.

No. No one got that much access to him. Never again.

"That's fine." She blew out a breath like she was relieved and stepped around the kitchen counter. "Can I grab something to eat before I lay down? I think my stomach would feel better with something on it."

Of course. A real gentleman would at least offer a glass of water to a young girl who'd been through some serious trauma. Especially if he was making her sleep on the couch.

He was born in the gutter, and one foot remained in it at all times. A tether not even he could undo.

"Help yourself. There's food in the fridge. Glasses in the cupboard."

"As they usually are. Not one for entertaining, huh?" Her struggle to keep the conversation light was palpable.

"I entertain nothing." Except fantasies of his family's tiny hovel burning to the ground while he held the smoking match. Only, someone else had beat him to it.

She laughed softly, her voice hoarse from her crying session. "I, for one, am shocked, Rourke. This place screams party city."

The corners of his mouth pulled down. His apartment was bare, necessary only to eat and sleep in. Was she teasing him?

"Relax, I'm giving you shit." She gave him a sad smile that didn't reach her red, puffy eyes. She busied herself filling glasses and pulling food out of the fridge. "I'm trying to keep my mind off everything, or I'll be locked in your bathroom all night. Well, it looks like we have water, wine and cold roast. Have you ever heard of vegetables?"

Why would he waste his time? "I haven't met a vegetable with the decent amount of blood."

An exasperated, forlorn sigh slipped out of her. "You're totally not what I thought you'd be."

Rourke cocked his head at the question. "What does that mean?"

She paused briefly before resuming meal prep. "You weren't exactly cracking jokes when we first met."

His senses prickled. She wasn't lying, but she wasn't forthcoming. He hadn't met her before tonight. He'd remember her. She slid a plate across the counter and set a glass of wine down. Since Grace stood on the kitchen side of his counter where he normally stood when he ate, he planted himself across from her and remained standing. There was a barstool, but he never cared for lingering over food.

Grace sliced a chunk of roast beef and slid it between her lips. His eyes followed the fork, lingering on her mouth. She caught him and feathered her fingers around her lips, searching the counter.

"Do you have a napkin?"

He'd allow her to assume that was why he'd been staring. A female eating shouldn't be fascinating, and he shouldn't be enthralled.

"In the drawer to your left." He sawed through his roast. The patience it required was always a challenge in self-discipline. To this day, decades after his captivity, each meal was a test in not shoveling food into his mouth by hand. Using utensils, even a plate, was a conscious decision every minute he ate.

Rourke didn't hide from his past. Acknowledging the atrocities he had survived prevented him from retreating into a shell of himself. Yes, he ate meals with others, but they weren't from his private food supply. Not if he could help it. Sharing his food with Grace was only another test.

Grace pulled out a black cloth napkin and dabbed at her mouth before taking a sip of wine. She continued tackling her roast, and he continued watching the fork slide through those lush pink lips.

Suddenly, sharing his food mattered less, not when he could do it with her.

"Oh, before I forget." She reached into her pocket and drew out the lock pick. "You'll find more out about this than I can."

How correct she was. Rourke deftly accepted the pick, avoiding skin contact.

She drained her wine and set her dishes by the sink. "I need to lie down."

Rourke waited until she exited the kitchen before he placed his dishes next to hers. Two sets of dirty flatware and glasses. A first for his pad.

He passed through the living room. Grace stared down at his couch. The reality of spending the night with a female under his roof dawned on Rourke. His strides quickened until he entered his bedroom and closed the door to block her presence out.

If his gut wasn't telling him she was so damn important to the case, he would've had Betty set up a guest room on the opposite end of headquarters.

A knock on the door snapped him around. He swore. Now she surprised him in his own home. Perhaps he should bypass Betty and set Grace up in another area himself.

"What?" he snarled.

"Dude, sorry." Her flippant tone suggested he no longer intimidated her the way he had earlier. He was both pleased and vexed by that. "Can I get a blanket and a pillow?"

Of course. Another hospitality fail. From his closet, he chose a fleece blanket riddled with penguins Zoey had thought was a hilarious gift for each member of the team and a knitted midnight blue throw—Betty's attempt at adding color into his life. He had no extra pillows. The only choice was one from the stack on his bed.

He held the blankets and glared at the innocent pillow. Once she used it, he doubted he could add it back to his collection.

She waited patiently. He opened the door and thrust the pile into her arms. Before she said her thanks, he shut the door.

"Thanks," she called extra loudly.

Another almost-smile twitched his lips. The girl had attitude if nothing else.

Chapter Three

Bishop shucked the shovel back into the Otto's car. Dawn was approaching and he still had to take the car to get it crushed.

Digging a grave for three adult bodies should've depleted his energy sources, but his restless spirit had been cooped up too long. That demon bitch called for him day and night, but tonight she'd been blessedly quiet, allowing him to actually be a functioning member of his team instead of expending energy ignoring her summons.

He didn't even know her name, didn't know who to curse. Only knew she had inhabited some poor human woman's body and used it to seduce him into binding himself to her. No idea what her bidding was, but he didn't intend to cross paths with her to find out. At least their bond didn't turn him into a puppet.

Her siren call in a throaty voice full of sexual promise was damn hard to resist. His determination to keep his distance might wither him into a pile of bones, but he'd do it. Like many, his demon probably assumed his physical size meant he lacked in mental capacity.

He checked his phone to see if his contact had gotten his message to meet him at the scrapyard. Nothing yet.

As he drove back to Freemont, his thoughts returned to the family he'd put in the ground. The poor girl. Grace. She exuded innocence, and he'd left her at Rourke's mercy. His buddy would never hurt her—physically. Rourke only inflicted pain on willing participants, but with a delicate bird like Grace, he didn't possess the empathy or tact to properly deal with her.

Bishop hoped the girl had the ability to handle her grief solo because there'd be no assistance from Rourke. In fact, Bishop would ensure he became Rourke's wingman on the investigation into the human family. Not just out of curiosity about a human family who willingly raised a vampire child, but because Grace brought out his brotherly urges. Feelings he only had for his team, and Demetrius's mate, Calli. His family.

Perhaps it was because Grace had lost her family, the pain fresh in her eyes, and he knew exactly how she felt.

Checking his phone again, he swore. No reply. He had two hours, max, before he needed to protect himself from daylight. His powerful prime vampire DNA could withstand the early morning rays of the sun. He'd give it more time. Bishop found a diner on the edge of town and pulled in.

As a large male, he'd never turn down a chance to devour bacon and eggs, and twenty-four hour diners such as this one knew how to serve 'em. His stomach rumbled in anger, insisting it craved blood.

He hadn't fed since that night the demon enslaved him. His team would gladly offer up a vein, but then he'd have to explain why he wasn't hitting up clubs for the last few weeks to find a willing and unwitting blood donor. And he couldn't reciprocate. The demon bond might've tainted his blood—it'd give him away.

Customers came and went from these kind of places. He could lure one of them to the dark edges of the parking lot and feed if he had to.

He ducked under the entrance into the restaurant, his large frame brushing the sides of the door. The tray in the young server's hand wobbled at his appearance. She was an attractive little thing, but that was the problem. She was tiny. Women with large frames and some meat on their bones were the only ones he hunted. They fulfilled his appetites more than one way.

Flashing her a pleasant smile, he ordered.

Bishop obsessively checked his messages until the food arrived ten minutes later. Still no response. He'd probably be bringing the Otto's vehicle home with him to scrap when the sun set again. Not ideal, but with Grace in their custody, the family shouldn't be reported missing anytime soon.

He polished off the last of his meal and threw a fifty down when another customer entered. He quickly slumped back into the booth.

If he were on the hunt for a woman tonight, she'd be it. Buxom blonde in a white wrap dress, she exuded Marilyn Monroe, only five inches taller. She glanced down both stretches on either side of the door, her expression distraught, and stumbled to the counter to sit across from him.

Her back offered a fine view. Her lushly rounded ass perched on the stool. Her legs crossed and curled underneath.

He frowned. Her body shook as if she were crying. Damn his soft heart.

Stay out of it. Resolute, he stood just as she turned with a shuddering cry.

Her watery gaze caught his eye. "Oh, sorry."

He needed to mind his own business, but felt caught, wishing to cheer her up. Then his body firmly reminded him it'd been weeks since his last woman and blood meal. He gestured for her to go ahead. "Ladies first."

"Oh." She sniffled, hastily wiping her eyes. "I was heading to the bathroom. I didn't mean to cut you off."

"It's no problem, really." He motioned for her to continue on to the bathroom.

She kept talking instead, leaving him frozen in place. Being rude wasn't in his nature. He was the vampire version of a teddy bear, unless he dealt with threats to helpless creatures. He forced himself to pay attention to what she was saying so he could extract himself from this situation.

"I mean, I keep calling him and he doesn't answer. When I try to meet him, he stands me up." She grabbed a tissue from her purse and dabbed at her eyes. "I'm worth more than that, right?"

"Of course," he answered automatically. He flicked his eyes toward the door and back to her. "I'd better get going."

"Oh, yes. Here I am making a nuisance of myself. You're probably thinking that guy is totally justified in ignoring me."

Bishop hesitated. He couldn't leave her like this. "Perhaps he's not worthy of you."

Her expression transformed until she beamed at him. "You're sweet." Tucking her hand into his elbow, she smiled sweetly. "Will you walk me out? I came in here to drown my sorrows in pancakes with whipped cream, but I have a better idea."

Her warmth seeped through his sleeve. Bishop gave himself a quick body scan, wondering how much dried blood was smeared over his clothes. His dark clothing concealed most of it, but a fine layer of dust from grave digging clung to his clothing. She didn't seem to mind.

They walked out together, but when he moved toward the sedan, her grip tightened.

"Can you walk me to my vehicle? It's still dark." Her voice held an edge of unease.

It was darkest before the dawn. "Where is it?"

She pointed to edge of the parking lot where it bordered a brick building. She'd chosen the corner where even light from the streetlamps didn't reach.

What had he pondered earlier? Luring a blood meal to the darkest section of the lot?

He couldn't let the opportunity pass.

Changing course, he accompanied her to the driver's side of her Jeep. He'd seduce her until she dropped her guard, and then sink his teeth into her soft creamy flesh. One mind wipe later, he'd be on his way well before the first rays of the sun brightened the sky.

She stalled at the driver's door and swung to face him, peering shyly up at him through her lashes. "Thank you."

Her desire wafted to his nose, sweet like the whipped cream she mentioned earlier. He may get more than a blood meal.

"My pleasure," he rumbled.

As he leaned down to capture her lips, she stood on her tiptoes and threw her arms around his neck. He fell into her, his arms wrapping around her waist. The salt of her tears seasoned her kiss. He lapped up the remnants of her sadness. Her body would sate his physical discomfort in several ways. The least he could do was leave her feeling good.

The way her she nipped and licked at him, he'd be more than fine when they were done. He barely registered her opening the back door and shoving him around. Their kiss broke only as she pushed him down into the seat.

"Lean back, big guy," she purred.

Oh, okay. She was going to take the lead. He could roll with that.

He scooted back so she could climb over him and wrestle the door shut behind them. The dome light went out and they were concealed once more. His superior vision wasn't affected. He could see everything, from her pink, passion tinted cheeks, to her ample cleavage spilling out of her dress.

She clawed at his pants, and he dimly wondered if she'd noticed his grime covered outfit at all. If she had, it certainly didn't slow her.

His shaft came to life. By the time she freed it, he was hard and ready to go. Biting her bottom lip, she eyed it greedily.

Bishop was pretty grateful his junkyard contact had stood him up. He'd scrap the car the next night.

As her hand glided up his cock, he groaned. At the top, she squeezed and pumped.

"Woman, it's not your hand I want." Hand jobs were nice and all, but it was easier to feed when she was in the throes of passion.

Misinterpreting his words, she slithered back as far as possible and licked her lips. She dipped her head down. His hips jerked up as her mouth wrapped around his shaft.

Hellfire. This isn't what he meant, either, but a few minutes wouldn't hurt.

He was a large man. Taller than most vampires and shifters, wider than any pro football player. The same went for his manhood. As her mouth stretched wide, she licked and sucked the tip. She wouldn't fit too much more inside.

Nope, wrong. The woman deep throated him like a pro.

His head fell back against the door, his eyelids closed. Only to pop open because it'd be a shame to miss the erotic show she put on with her ass pressed against the window across from him. He marveled over women. Some almost conducted background checks before they allowed him to touch their bodies. Some, like the siren blowing him, jumped in without even an introduction.

Her hot tongue slid over him as she increased suction. One release before she rode him wouldn't hurt.

As his balls tightened, she hummed.

His orgasm built—only to be shut down. She released him with a pop and grinned wickedly. His release slinked back where it came from. She sucked him back into her mouth.

The routine continued until he bellowed with physical pain when she teased his orgasm one last time.

He was *so fucking close*, as soon as her breath blew over his cock, he'd blow.

He was a large print book, she read him easily. Crawling up his body, she hovered over him.

She wasn't wearing underwear. How desperate was this chick?

The brief concern of using a condom was stamped out when her liquid heat encompassed him. She slid slowly, moans of frustration escaping her.

"I want to slam down on you, but this body can't handle all of you so suddenly."

Desperate and talking in third person—Bishop tried not to care. She was crazy, but her blood would flow red. Except...a warning bell dinged. Hadn't he experienced this before?

Finally, she sunk down all the way, swiveling her hips to adjust. His mind was ripped back to her, to them. The way she'd played with him, he'd last two seconds before he exploded.

A lazy grin spread across her face. "That's more like it. You want it don't you?"

He nodded. She rose up and slammed back down. The breath whooshed out of him. Twice more and he was ready to come, but he wanted her to climax as he sunk his teeth in.

His thumb found her nub. She freed her breasts, thumbing her nipples.

Crazy and hot. Crazy hot.

"Look me in the eyes, baby." With his other hand, he cupped her chin to mesmerize her.

She met his gaze squarely. "No, Bishop, you look."

He froze, but she rode him. His body ignored his mind to abort mission.

"How do you know my name?" He tried to release her mound.

She shook her head, an iron grip holding his hand in place at her sex. "You've been a naughty boy, ignoring me."

It was *her*. He'd been tricked—again.

"What are you?" he snarled.

Her walls tightened around him and his orgasm burst forth. Clenching his teeth, gritting his eyes shut, he couldn't fight it. Pleasure poured through him, out doing the humiliation at being tricked by the demon bitch yet again.

Her cries broke through his as she hit her own peak.

Scrambling to recover, he cleared his lust-hazed thoughts to confront her.

Her hand yanked a fistful of his hair, her face inches from his, her eyes completely black. "This is the way it's going to play, Bishop. *You. Are. Mine*. You swore yourself to me. I'm generous. I'll give you one week to gather up all the information your team knows, and you'll meet me at the first place we had sex." She released him and sat up, circling her pelvis, calling his shaft back to attention. "In return, I'll serve all your needs."

"This body is not yours." The young woman she possessed had no say in what the demon did to its host.

The demoness shrugged. "She knew what she was agreeing to when she volunteered to host me." She broke into a wicked grin. "I may have omitted a few details. I choose what you like, Bishop."

"I won't do it," he gritted between his teeth. Her body or not, he couldn't seem to control his reaction. Another orgasm was knocking on his balls.

She leaned over him and drew his face into her neck. "You will because I told you to. You said the oath. Now drink. I'm ready to come."

His fangs were bared and buried before his conscience could chime in.

They both climaxed, his one of the hardest he'd ever experienced.

His fangs disengaged and his muscles bunched, prepared to throw her off.

Her cool fingers feathered over his forehead. "I don't think so, big guy. I need you to sleep."

Heavy eyelids proved impossible to fight. What kind of power did the demoness possess? As he drifted off, he heard her say, "Wake in ten minutes, my goliath. I don't want you burning that handsome face of yours in the sun."

***

Grace's eyes fluttered open, she sat up with a gasp. Her gaze landed on Rourke, standing over her frowning. His arms were crossed over his cut chest, leaving washboard abs visible until they disappeared into the low-slung waistband of gray flannel sweats. Obsidian eyes glittered in the faint light emanating from his bedroom. She sucked in a breath. Only the idea that he slept with a nightlight contained the scream in her throat.

Remnants of dual nightmares faded away. Images of her birth family and Rourke wandering through their remains to her human family spread in a bloody line before him.

To wake up to the male looming over her…she gulped. She should be terrified. She should've yelled. Instead, his presence calmed her as it fired up all her fantasies. Warmth spread through her, moving farther down.

"What are you doing?" She croaked out the question in her attempt to disengage her mind from the hormones it spurred through her body.

"You were making noise." His tone lacked inflection in the usual Rourke way.

Flashes of her dead families continued to storm through her brain. She rubbed her temples and pinched the bridge of her nose to keep from crying. When she peered back up at him, she released a frustrated huff at his pained expression. "Are you afraid I'm going to cry again?"

Wariness settled into his gaze. "It would be understandable."

How could she be afraid of a male whose distress stemmed from the expectation she might need his comfort?

"No, Rourke. I'm not going to cry, again." She gave herself a mental shake. No more breakdowns. She swung her legs down and hauled herself up. "It wouldn't do any good anyway."

His eyes roamed her face, lifted to skim over her hair.

She patted her wild mane. To sleep comfortably, she'd taken out her hair tie. "My curls go a little crazy when they're not contained."

He kept eyeing her hair. Grace dug into her pants pocket for her tie. His hand snaked around her wrist, encasing it in an iron grip.

"Don't." He was close enough she could make out the subtle difference between the black pupil and rich brown iris. "Your hair…it's like strands of rich caramel dancing in firelight."

What sensual words. Her gaze locked onto his. She lost herself in the depths of wonder she saw there. How could her unbound, crazy hair undo this male?

He leaned in, his slightly parted lips and hypnotic hooded gaze short-circuited her brain. She pressed up and their lips met. His gentle touch packed such magnitude it rocked the foundation of her being. Since she was old enough to form memories, she'd been afraid of this male. Now he touched her hair, gave her a chaste kiss, and she handed herself over to him?

Before she could sort through her thoughts, the kiss deepened. His thumb caressed her wrist, setting every nerve ablaze. Tentatively, his tongue swiped out. She opened for him, accepting his offer to deepen contact. Their tongues swirled in mutual discovery. His rich taste like a strong coffee—she was immediately addicted.

She rose on her tiptoes to wrap her arms around his shoulders. He stiffened. Her body rebelled when she pulled back, but Rourke's discomfort kicked in her nurturing instincts. As the kiss broke, his tongue scraped against one of her fangs. A drop of his blood touched her tongue and she moaned. Her hands dug into his shoulders and her blood hunger roared to life.

Suddenly her feet swooped off the floor as he shoved her onto the couch.

Her eyes flew open. "What the hell?"

"Don't touch me." His snarl unveiled deadly fangs.

Subtle vibrations wracked his body. Rage filled his features, red stained his cheeks—whether it was from anger or lust, she didn't know. His body taut, he leaned over her, his pupils blown so wide she feared she'd see the fires of Hell in them. She shrank back into the cushions.

"Never," his voice shook with barely contained fury, "*never* take my blood."

He spun on his heel and stormed to his room, slamming the door.

Grace exhaled a shaky breath and drew her legs up to her chest. That was a hell of reaction to an accident. Where did his rage stem from?

The Rourke she'd gotten to know the last twenty hours had seemed at odds with her nightmare vampire. The Rourke who left the room fit him perfectly.

What was she going to do? She had no idea if she was in the home of a killer.

No doubt he *was* a killer, but was he the one who murdered her family? Was he the male from her dream?

The whoosh of the bedroom door opening reached her ears. Out walked a fully dressed Rourke with his ink black hair slicked back off his face. A jaw-dropping, debonair male dressed in a quality sweater and gray slacks who knew how good he looked.

"Get cleaned up. You have a meeting with Demetrius. He'll be here in two minutes."

He stepped into the hallway without glancing back.

"Wha—what the fuck?" she shouted at the closed door. "Asshole."

No reply. He called his boss rather than face her after an accidental exchange of *one* drop of his blood? Perhaps he was too cowardly to have been the killer after all.

Chapter Four

The dimly lit country club oozed refined class. Conversations murmured amongst the clientele resembled negotiations. Members of vampire prime families roamed from table to mahogany table, designer labels and custom garments hugged their lithe frames. Piano music topped off the upscale atmosphere.

It was all about appearance, Rourke mused. Wearing his own charcoal cashmere sweater and black slacks with a crisp seam, he fit in with the crowd mulling about.

He despised them all. Vampires who were born with money, prestige, secreting themselves into these private clubs where they could debauch among their own kind. Then gaze down upon all the lower-born vampires with derision and distain.

No wonder they had a demon problem. Vampire arrogance thinking they could control something as powerful as the friggin' underworld.

Rourke nodded to acquaintances, some former sexual partners. Despite their come hither coy glances, he was only interested in one female in particular.

And it wasn't Grace-fucking-Otto.

No one took his blood without permission. Not anymore. *Not ever*. Just the thought of her fang nicking him bombarded his mind with overwhelming lust for the lovely female that heightened the nauseating pit in his stomach. For a split second when it had happened, he'd wanted to groan in ecstasy. Until the soul-deep memories that plagued him made him want to retch instead.

Hellfire, he'd thrown her. What if there hadn't been a couch there? Her body hitting the wall would've sickened him worse than the blood exchange had.

No, not an exchange. He hadn't given his permission all the times before with others more brutal, more uncaring than Grace. In her eyes, it'd been an accident. To him, it'd always be a violation. The last vampires who drank from him without permission had suffered at his hand—and boots and fangs—for days before they dusted in the sunlight.

Grace experiencing any pain from him...Rourke's stomach twisted. He hated what she'd done, yet his body pleaded for her to drink from him. Being away from her right now drove him *freaking* crazy, but he couldn't stand the thought of facing her. He was on fire, his insides turned on like he'd *never* known, but his past continuously fed him chunks of his enslavement until he wanted to kneel down and vomit on someone's wingtips.

Rourke located the female he searched for. Game face in place, he made his way toward her table. She swiveled in her high-back chair toward him, sensing his presence. A demure smile twisted her painted red lips. A cascade of midnight curls partially obscured the pale arch of her slender neck. He'd fed long and often from the blue-tinged vein peeking through her hair. All while she had been restrained in the harness that hung from the ceiling of one of the private guest rooms.

Everyone else faded to the periphery of his vision and his focus narrowed on her.

"Manka," he growled once he reached her side.

She gazed up at him, a hitch in her breath, waiting only for him to ask.

"I have four sets of padlocks and an empty table. Are you available?"

***

A knock on the door sounded before a male's voice spoke. "Open up, Grace. It's Demetrius."

Grace opened the door to a pair of pale green eyes steeped in pity. The reason for the sympathy could be from many things. Losing her vampire family, then her human family. How Rourke couldn't get away from her fast enough.

"Come with me," was all he said before heading down the hall.

She scurried after him, following through the maze of corridors.

"If Rourke didn't fill you in, I'm from a prime family." Demetrius didn't turn his head, kept it succinct. "My team and I destroyed the Vampire Council. Now I sit on the TriSpecies Synod and help govern all the non-humans."

Whoa. Not just anyone took her in. Rourke and Bishop must be part of his team. Made sense they were the ones investigating possible demon interference. Once they reached a room where a beautiful female with hair the color of sunshine waited, Demetrius ushered her inside and closed the door.

"Callista," Demetrius said, "this is Grace."

"Call me Calli." Her expression matched her mate's I'm-sorry-you-experienced-something-shitty one. But hers came across as more…knowing. A quality that endeared Grace to her immediately.

Grace would love to have someone she could call a friend. She would love to have someone, period. Nathaniel had been her best friend. As a vampire, she couldn't garner human friendships, and she hadn't known any other vampires.

Her gaze flitted around the meeting room. The contemporary style with sleek lines and polished surfaces contradicted her stereotype of old-world vampires. But it fit the couple who sat in it with her.

Demetrius slid a water bottle in front of Grace.

"Tell us anything and everything, Grace." Calli opened a notepad and clicked a pen. "If you don't mind, I'd like to take notes. I've been studying demons and I don't want to miss something crucial."

"Go for it, but I don't have much to spill. Sometimes, I wonder if I formed a false memory." *Until I laid eyes on Rourke and déjà vu kicked me in the ass.* "My birth parents had been slaughtered, just senseless. I can recall what the room looked like. Every detail. It was a simple room, with normal furniture, no different than what I had growing up with my human family."

"By normal, you mean what?" Demetrius asked.

"Middle class. My mom worked as a teller at a bank. My dad managed a convenience store."

Calli glanced at Demetrius. "She's not prime?"

He inclined his head. "It's a safe assumption. You know what prime means? You didn't question it when I mentioned it before."

"No, my parents told me all about vampires and shifters and the bad guys who hunted them."

"The ones I destroyed." He stated it, no gloating, just reality.

Geez, who was she hanging around?

"And they knew all that how?" He calmly regarded her, but his scrutiny was palpable.

Grace shrugged. "I never questioned them. I mean, parents know everything, except during our teenage years when they know nothing. Vampires have that too, right?"

Calli smirked. "They never grow out of it."

Grace expected Demetrius to scowl, but his lips twisted in an arrogant smile at his mate's joke.

They reminded her of her parents. The love between them had been strong and clear, but they had constantly ribbed each other.

She missed them so much. A wave of sorrow hit her, she dropped her gaze from them.

"I'm sorry." Callie dropped her pen to lay her hand on Grace's.

"It doesn't seem possible." Words poured from Grace's mouth. "It was literally last night I talked to them. And my brother. He's like my twin. He never thought I was weird or resented keeping my secret. He always said it was cool as shit his big sis was a vampire. Now their bodies are buried who knows where. Actually, the giant does."

Grace sniffled and a tissue appeared in front of her. Calli thought of everything. Perhaps she'd experienced similar tragedy.

Wiping her nose, she continued her cathartic word vomit. "I was homeschooled. Not like you can send a vampire to public school. Mom hated teaching. She was impatient, but she'd always say, 'It's not you, dear, it's me. I suck at this.' She'd do it after working a full day. Dad helped me find colleges with online programs. It was fucking hard, because what degree will give me a job I can do from home? But I learned how not to teach from Mom. I became an online instructor to use my skills." Grace's laugh echoed false in her own ears.

Demetrius's brows drew down. "How did they send you to college? Fake documents to enroll you?"

"I guess. Dad taught me how to drive and then came home with a driver's license for me one day."

He sat back, considering the information. "Have you lived in Freemont your whole life?"

"My parents bought the house when my brother and I were very young and we've lived there ever since."

"They had a contact to supply them with fake documents then."

Grace's papers for anything had been fake, of course. She'd never considered her family's documents were also fake. While she was growing up, they hadn't acted paranoid, but then it'd been over twenty years since they'd settled in the house in Freemont. It was her home. Her parents were her parents. She was a normal online vampire tutor raised by humans.

Calli filled in the pause while Demetrius frowned at the tabletop. "Is there anything unusual you remember before tonight? Any reason why your family was targeted?"

Grace shook her head, helpless as ever. "It seems there's a lot they didn't tell me. If they ran across trouble, I was left out of it."

Demetrius pushed back. "It's time we search your house."

Calli passed Grace another reassuring look. "Are you ready? You're welcome to stay here while we go."

"I want to be involved. I need to be useful." *I need to find who did this.*

"I understand. Can you flash us there?" Calli watched her expectantly.

Grace blinked. Could she? "Do you guys need to grab anything first?"

She asked to totally buy time because she didn't want to admit she didn't flash often, didn't flash long distances, and never attempted to bring anyone. Except one time she flashed with Nathaniel to avoid getting caught drinking by her parents. She flashed them from the fire pit to the upper level of their house when they'd heard their parents drive up. An ingenious move—if the fire hadn't still been burning with their liquor sitting out. Nathaniel had been fully human, so flashing with two vampires who could also flash was entirely possible in her new world.

"I'm always locked and loaded." Demetrius waited with his arms folded. Calli stood next to him, both of them patient as if they knew it was a difficult decision for Grace.

"Do you follow me or do we need to hold hands or something."

Calli extended her hand for Grace to grab. "We don't have Rourke's talent of tracing a flashing path."

"Rourke's a full bucket of surprises." Grace's sarcasm-laced words shocked her. She'd actually spoken that shit out loud.

Demetrius barked a laugh. Grace pictured her house and flashed.

Chapter Five

R ourke considered the female before him, waiting for her answer. It'd be yes. Her craving for hard sex was as strong as his urge to tie up his sexual partner. They made a great pair. But that wasn't the reason he'd approached her tonight.

"Of course, Rourke. You know I'd never turn you down." Manka uncrossed her legs. The site of her damp sex peeking out from beneath her ultra-short skirt was supposed to turn him on.

It had before. Likely due to the business he had with her. The sight of her glistening flesh did nothing now. Tonight, he could be examining a lettuce salad on a full stomach. His hunger gnawed at him, but the idea of feeding from Manka left him as nauseous as eating out of restaurant garbage bins. He'd know.

He inclined his head, acknowledging the view. A seductive smile lifted her shiny red lips, and she stood up. He trailed her sexy saunter to a private room. No lights, no windows, just a pain-pleasure sanctuary for those inclined.

Rourke's tastes didn't drift that way. He only craved controlling the level of intimacy until he had full control. If he could feed from himself, then he and his hand would survive just fine. He'd think of another outlet for his lock-picking hobby.

Manka slid into the swing chair suspended from the ceiling. She tucked her feet into the dangling foot straps and threaded her arms into the restraints. Rourke prowled around her, securing buckles—their usual routine.

Her shellacked lips pouted. "Rourke, where's your enthusiasm? You're usually at least half-mast by now."

He ruthlessly yanked the last buckle tight. She gasped and her eyes glazed over in desire. "We need to clear the air first, Manka."

Her expression turned questioning and impatient. "We don't waste much time talking."

"No." He wandered to the wall to pretend to select his toy. "And I'm hoping we won't waste much time today."

Because the longer he was away from Grace, the worse he itched under the collar. Wanted to go find her.

Ridiculous.

She meant nothing to him other than a means to solve a case, regardless if his body still sang for her bite.

Impatience won. He gave up his pretense and ambled to Manka's side to loom over her.

He lifted her wrist to his mouth. She writhed, sending waves of lust over him. Intent on his mission, he nicked her skin and let a drop of blood touch his tongue.

The urge to gag overwhelmed him. After what he investigated the previous night, the taste of her blood was revolting yet very telling.

His anger bloomed in the room. Now she realized he released no stench of arousal.

"Rourke?" Her muscles bunched as she strained against her bonds. A hint of fear laced her voice. "What's going on?"

"I think you know." He gazed impassively down at her. "Talk, Manka. Why did you steal from me?"

Her breath caught and she drew her limbs into herself, seeking protection. "I wanted a memento of our time together."

The acrid taste of a lie stained her scent. "Bullshit."

"Rourke, darling. It was just a tiny thing." Manka's breathing quickened. "I didn't think you'd miss it." She wasn't lying. In her mind, she believed what she'd done was no big.

"Who asked you to do it?" His voice was soft, almost holding a hint of compassion while there really was none.

Her lips quivered. "I don't know what you're talking about. I wanted a memento of our time together."

"For fuck's sake, Manka, I can smell your lie."

A hard glint entered her eyes. "I won't tell you anything other than he told me you weren't born prime." Her mouth twisted in a sneer. "You claim I lie, but you waltz in here, acting as if you belong with us. We let you inside of us when you're nothing but a commoner."

His heart thudded once, twice. He held himself back from striking the wall.

Nothing but a commoner.

If only. He was much lower than that. "Yet you were wet before we even got in here."

She bared her fangs. "The damage is already done. You're at least good enough for a fuck."

Any emotion he'd generated in her presence drained away. One night long ago, he'd sworn to himself he would be used for more than fucking or feeding. That night had started with him escaping his restraints and ended with blood on his hands. And his face. And his clothing until there was nothing left of his master to splatter.

He'd honor his oath and bring Manka to justice. A twofer. "Did you participate?"

She stilled, her creamy complexion draining to ashen. "I don't know what you're talking about."

His hunch had been correct. "Good try. Your lies stink. I smell their deaths lingering in your blood. I hope your last meal was filling."

Punishing Manka would only bring a modicum of justice for Grace. Manka was a tool. The vampire who had set her up held all the blame.

But Manka still had to pay. He walked to the door and knocked twice. It swung open to reveal Zohana.

"Manka, have you met Zoey?"

Manka's conniving expression fell and filled with dawning horror.

"Yes, it's serious." Rourke nodded to Zoey and stepped back.

Zoey's doe brown eyes rested on Manka. "Crimes against any species, but especially humans, threaten all our kind. You aided in the murder of three humans. The sentence is death. Care to share who else was involved?"

A glob of spit landed at Zoey's shoe.

That would be no.

Zoey's expression hardened. "I'll take care of this prime filth, Rourke. Go find the bastard behind this."

He tensed as Manka opened her mouth. He prepared for obscenities about his origin in front of a female he considered a friend.

Zoey's fist moved faster than he registered. Manka's head snapped back, the restraints held her body in place.

"If you're going to waste air saying something, make sure it's about why you attacked the human family."

Manka spit blood. The foamy glob landed at Zoey's feet. Despite her restraints, Manka smiled without a care in the world. Black ebbed into her eyes.

"Shit." Zoey withdrew a wooden stake from her knee-high boot.

Manka's eyes widened and her smile turned into a sneer. The hairs on the back of Rourke's neck stood up. A gust of wind buffeted through the room—the completely closed in room. He lunged for Manka to stop the demon from summoning its power just as Zoey's arm snapped up and crashed the stake down into Manka's chest.

The restraints swung empty. Dusted. It had happened so fast, the image of the demon possessing Manka hung in her place.

Rourke opened the door. "Get out of here, Zoey."

They rushed out as the gaping hole formed under the apparition to claim it back for Hell. The roar of an air tunnel sounded as the door slammed shut. Rourke only hoped the pile of Manka's dust survived to leave a message to anyone else involved.

***

Grace sat in her bedroom, clutching a neon pink duffel bag with black piping. Calli had suggested she collect a few items and pack a bag.

Then she'd broken the news it was no longer Grace's home, which she had already gathered from Rourke. Sucked to have it confirmed. After they finished tonight, Demetrius would send a vampire crew to clean it out and sell it. Just like that, her family's existence would be gone.

She blew out a heavy breath. Part of her wanted to rail against the powers that be. Scream and shout and throw heavy objects while she declared how utterly unfair it all was. The other half was relieved to not have to deal with clearing out her loved ones' belongings. This wasn't emptying a room or cleaning out a closet—all terrible enough. Emptying a house and moving on lifted the pain to unmanageable, unthinkable, levels. And Grace didn't know if she possessed the strength to do it, and she would've had to do it alone because she was the only one left.

Dropping the duffel that was too cheery for the situation, Grace began to pack. Rolling clothing to stuff into the corners, she filled the bag and went in search of her backpack. Vampires weren't known for international travel and neither were her parents—that she knew of—so a nice suitcase wasn't available. Grace unhooked her laptop, wrapped up the cords and stashed it in its case. Only two pictures, one with all four of them and the other with just her and Nathaniel, stood on her nightstand. Into the backpack those went.

Done. Her life boiled down to two bags and laptop. Were other vampires like this? Grace guessed her packed possessions surpassed Rourke's.

Rourke. Her anger at the way he dumped her on the couch almost exceeded her irritation she didn't know where he went. One drop of blood and he disappeared. Not that they'd connected.

Except for that confusing gentle kiss—a contradiction compared to the intense male. In his initial hesitance, she'd sensed a deep need to be accepted, to not be rejected, yet fear she wouldn't push him away.

It was what? A ten second kiss? And it branded its way into her heart more than any other boyfriend she'd ever had.

Humans. Maybe that was the difference. Two were tame guys she'd met, online of course, where she could control the interaction and get a good sense of their unstable quotient. The third was one of Nathaniel's friends. Dating him had made her brother nervous, but Grace had assured him the relationship was slightly more than a fling. More a reprieve from the physical loneliness that sometimes plagued her. Once his friend's feelings delved deeper, she cut it off, leaving him disappointed and her with a tinge of regret.

Demetrius had inquired about her past, and she was resolute none of her three exes had anything to do with the tragedy. All breakups were amicable. Nathaniel's friend was even engaged to another girl already and Grace wished them well.

But one kiss from an unemotional stone usurped her whole dating existence. Her intuition urged her to keep trying, to not give up on the male who shoved her away and stalked out calm and collected. Her intuition should've told her to run from him, but his reaction was yet another discrepancy comparing him to her nightmare vision.

Demetrius and Calli's movements in the lower level prompted Grace to stay on the top floor and start her search in her parents' office. From there, she could search their bedroom and then her brother's bedroom.

Collecting her bags and dropping them at the top of the stairs, she wandered to the office. She lingered in the hall as she passed the photographs that lined the walls. Happy faces, happy times. She moved on before another bout of crying delayed her mission.

She paused after she entered the office. The eerie sense she intended to dig for dirt on her beloved parents upset her stomach. She shook it off. If it brought their killers to justice, she'd turn this house inside out.

She rifled through their desk, but found standard items: bills, receipts, ledgers. The filing cabinet held the usual offenders: tax returns, house repairs, owner's manuals. None of it did Grace any good other than reinforce the idea maybe her parents just innocuously knew vampires existed. And had enough knowledge to raise one, because who doesn't?

Redoubling her efforts, she pulled out drawers. Her fingers swiped around surfaces, her eyesight good enough to not require a flashlight. The filing cabinet held no hidden surprises. She focused on the desk, thinking about her next stop. Where was the best place to stash incriminating documents?

The left side of the desk was as typical as could be. The right side held a locked drawer Grace overpowered easily enough. With her strength, a forceful tug popped it open with a chuck of splintered wood hanging off the lock.

Bank documents. Normal ones at that.

Grace set the stash on the desk, huffing stray curls off her face. They were in their usual state of disarray if she didn't wear a headband or confine them to a clip. It was her favorite look really, but she tamed it when she recorded her lessons or Skyped with a student so she wasn't continually blowing them out of her eyes.

Glancing around at the scattered papers and drawers of various sizes, she liked the idea she didn't have to clean up after herself. She toed the locked drawer out of the way. It was then she registered something wasn't right. She squatted down, peered into where the drawer used to sit, felt around. Nothing unusual. She turned her attention back to the drawer.

Whaddya know? The interior of the drawer was not as deep as the opening it went into.

A zing of excitement raced through her. If someone was going to find something, she wanted it to be her.

She pushed and pried to figure out the opening mechanism. Where there was some give, she increased pressure and with a satisfying pop, the bottom compartment dumped papers onto the floor.

Eyes wide, she sat and spread out the documents. Three passports and a small notebook lay among the cache. Opening them all side by side, she recognized her parents, but not their names. The baby photo resembled pics she'd seen of Nathaniel as a baby, but again, different name.

The dates on the passports were mere weeks before they'd adopted her, and they were long past expired.

Holy shit, she'd been living with strangers. All three of them. What the hell would drive a couple with a baby to change their names? They were an everyday family, lived in the 'burbs, mowed their lawn on the weekend.

People changed identities when they were in trouble, or when they *were* the trouble.

She gathered up the papers and arranged them in a neat pile to scan one by one, saving the notebook for last. There were no more than ten papers, and they were mostly applications for fake documents. She set those aside for Demetrius.

Voices drifted in through the door just as she opened the notebook. She sensed the male who'd been troubling her all night before he strode in, appearing as unflappable as always and wearing the same clothing he left in.

"Seriously, Rourke. You should go home and change first." Demetrius kept pace behind him, but Rourke ignored him.

He pulled up short when his gaze landed on Grace. Her mind shorted and irrational anger swelled.

"Uck. You smell like sex. Get out with that whore stench on you." Rationally, Grace had nothing to be upset about. A kiss did not define a relationship, and his danger to her wellbeing hadn't been established.

Rourke being hot and heavy with *anyone* pissed her *the fuck* off. Then to have the brazen audacity to march into the same room with her? What. An. Ass.

"I didn't have sex." Rourke's cool mask slipped to reveal his disconcerted expression.

Ha! It didn't bother him that she was furious, but if she was tumbling in emotional turmoil, then she'd make sure he was, too.

"Then someone had sex *on* you. You stink. Get out." Grace snatched up her find, stood, and marched past Rourke, glaring into his dark, glittering eyes the entire way.

He tracked her as she handed the papers to Demetrius, kept the notebook for herself and left the office.

"Take the hint next time, Rourke," Demetrius muttered before she slammed the door to her parent's bedroom.

It wasn't enough to block the voices, unless Rourke intentionally spoke loud enough to carry across the wooden barrier.

"It shouldn't concern her whose sex I smell like."

"It obviously does. And after the call I got from you early this evening, you have shit with her to settle before you parade around your club habits."

"I told you what I was doing," Rourke growled.

"Yeah, just me." Demetrius's voice dropped until Grace strained to listen with her ear pressed to the door. "You're in charge of an investigation she's an integral part of. You can't have issues with her. I'm taking you off the case. Betty's set up another room for her."

"This is my case, Demetrius. You can't save the fucking world by yourself. It's a simple investigation. And Grace is staying with me."

"Why?"

Grace held her breath with Demetrius's question. Yes, why?

"Because."

She almost sputtered. He was infuriating! It aggrevated the hell out of her that she didn't want to move to another room either.

"Rourke," Demetrius's tone grew concerned, "I've never seen you this ruffled by a female." Grace's ego swelled, then her ire flattened it, remembering his stench. "Until we figure her out, Bishop should take point."

A low rumble rattled from Rourke. "Fine. She stays in another room, but I'm lead on this investigation."

Rather than have her work with another male? But he could go stir up a cloud of orgasm with another female?

"You will keep me updated every step of the way," Demetrius warned.

"When I do never update you?" Rourke retorted.

Papers rustled. They must be going through her discovery.

She tiptoed to her parents' king-sized bed so the males wouldn't know she'd eavesdropped. Once settled, she opened the notebook. Her instinct was to read through this alone.

Her mouth dropped open with a small gasp. Written in her mom's scrawl was a letter.

Dearest Children,

At the risk of sounding cliché, if you're reading this, we are most likely dead. If we aren't, then you're in serious trouble for snooping!

Whether we died of natural causes or nefarious ones, you both deserve to know the truth. I hoped one day we would've told you everything, but your father and I didn't want to upset the idyllic life we'd built.

You see, before you lovely children came along, our business was committing despicable acts. We worked for an organization that hunted supernatural creatures. We foolishly thought we were doing right by the world.

Our eyes were opened after several signs those we hunted were more decent than those we worked for.

If you found this stash, then you found the passports. Once we had our own child, we couldn't risk his safety and planned an escape using connections. Only we couldn't follow through—we were afraid. We went on one more mission.

That's where you come in, Grace. Your family was our target. I honestly can't tell you if we would've gone through with it, but when we arrived, they were already dead, except a precious little toddler survived.

You finalized our plans to get out, but we couldn't fly with you. You were a squirmy little bundle, and we doubted we could protect you from the light on a long trip. We fled to Freemont with you both, hoping it was a city large enough to get lost in, with enough vampires for Grace to blend.

Grace hiccupped around the tears rolling down her face. It killed her more the letter was addressed to both her and her brother, but he was gone, too. If her mom and dad had known it would end this way…

I wrote this so you'd know who we were. We were good people doing bad things for what we thought were the right reasons. That should make us bad people, but life's not clear cut, unfortunately.

Whether you read the next pages, I'll leave that up to you both. For my own sanity, I had to unload all of the atrocities we'd committed. A few of them may have benefitted the human population, but I'll never know for sure. And if I did know, I don't know that it'd make me feel better.

You both are worth the risk of leaving everything to raise you in the human world. Your father and I loved you with everything and were over the moon we got to experience a normal life with our children.

Love Mom and Dad.

Grace dropped the notebook, sobbing. It felt like all she was good for lately.

Dimly, she became aware of Rourke standing before her.

"God, you stink," she declared between sniffles.

"I didn't fuck her."

"Whatever. It's not my *concern*."

He frowned. Score one for Grace Otto. She cracked his expression again.

"The lock pick you found was mine, angel."

Her heart dropped to her toes. The clue at the crime scene incriminated him.

"I often…" His gaze dropped while he decided what to say. "I…dislike…being restrained. Therefore, I often practice my abilities to escape various restraints—without myself being in them. One of my previous partners stole the pick from me, and I narrowed it down to one female. My goal in seeing her tonight was to discover who she stole it for and why."

Grace squinted at his handsome features, trying to determine if she was interpreting him correctly. "Bondage?"

"For my partner."

"Our kiss must've been pretty vanilla compared to what you did tonight."

His eyes still hung on the floor, indecision in his features. "I don't kiss, Grace. Unless I'm ripping someone's throat out, I don't even touch."

She snorted. When he glanced at her in confusion, she rolled her eyes toward him. "You don't get drenched in sex without touching."

"The scent clings regardless. Some females react powerfully from their own fetishes."

"So you tied her up and gave her multiple orgasms? Tell me, Rourke, how does that interrogation technique work?"

His eyes lit with a menacing glow that stuttered her heart—*because she liked it*. "There were no orgasms tonight, nor will there be any more for her."

Holy shit. He said it in a tone that would've made Batman ask for advice. Suddenly, Grace pitied the female.

She made an attempt to soften the conversation. "What'd you find out?"

His expression darkened. "Whoever talked her into the task held more sway over her than I did."

"Why would you be framed?"

A scowl tightened his features. "I have no clue." He hesitated, and she knew she wouldn't like what he said next. "She helped kill your parents."

Oh. Her pity went up in flames. "Thank you for telling me."

His gaze dropped from hers, his only sign of relief. Had he been worried how she'd handle the news? Figuratively, she wanted to rip the female's heart out. Literally, she didn't know if she could do it. But one aspect of justice had been served and that eased a small fraction of her grief.

He stooped to pick up the notebook. She snatched it away. He gave her a sharp look and held his hand out.

"I don't know what's in here." What if her parents saw the same male she did that night? Would that be written in here?

The truth was, she couldn't read it. She dropped her gaze to the notebook. Her soul was shredded from the letter. Reading the entire notebook was a daunting task. She handed it over. Rourke accepted it and immediately paged through it.

Grace clasped her hands, fiddling her thumbs in a one-person thumb war. She turned her thoughts elsewhere to ignore the book Rourke held.

She might have a clue, and it might wreck her secret hunt for her vampire family's killers. But if it wasn't Rourke, he could help her.

"I have one memory before I was adopted. I don't even know if it's a memory." She sucked in a breath and rushed out, "You were walking among the remains of my parents."

Rourke stopped reading, surprise etched in his features.

"You can imagine why I kept flashing away from you when I saw you again among my parents' remains."

Several emotions traveled across his face until it matched the what-the-hell-do-we-make-of-that thoughts she'd been having the last day.

"It wasn't me," he said, simply.

"Rourke," Demetrius barked from the doorway, "we have reports of another human family targeted by vampires." He entered, warily glancing between the two.

She didn't know him well, but in the hours she had, he came across as the guy who trumped any conversation he declared necessary. It wasn't Grace's imagination something simmered between her and Rourke, not after she heard their discussion and the way Demetrius approached to avoid interrupting.

"Tell him," Rourke ordered.

She should rise. She had to crane her neck up to see them both, but she didn't get up. Already exposed and raw, relating the dream that had haunted her for her whole life sapped her energy.

Demetrius's brows rose as she spilled the details. A second telling was as cathartic as the first. More so, because he was a third party and that validated the terror she'd grown up with. Between her and Rourke, it was a haunting event, but the more she vocalized her recurring nightmare, the more substance it had.

Rourke passed the notebook to Demetrius who took his turn paging through it. Grace cringed. They read her parents' deepest, darkest secrets, and she'd only just met the males. Her hand twitched to snatch it away. If she hadn't sensed their vested interest in solving the murders, she might have.

Demetrius whistled. "Damn. Does she relate the details of the night Grace was orphaned?"

"Let me see." Rourke flicked to the end of the journal and took a moment to read. His brows shot up. "They left a nice detail."

Grace's interest perked.

"Shiiit." Demetrius called over his shoulder. "Callista."

The blonde raced in as Grace demanded, "*What?*"

Rourke answered her as Demetrius and Calli murmured over the notebook. "They mentioned being worried the vampires were going to burn the place if they didn't find you. Because it smelled like matches."

Grace shot up. "Sulfur! Demons were behind both sets of murders? How could they *not* be related?"

"Very possible," Calli agreed. "But we don't want to pigeonhole ourselves with assumptions. Demons are devious."

Rourke nodded. "Wanna bet this third murder scene has a sulfur taint?"

"Or another piece of evidence incriminating you," Grace added.

He paused as if he hadn't thought of that.

At Calli's questioning look, Demetrius filled her in on Grace's dream.

"It's an awful coincidence both Grace and Rourke are linked to each scene." Calli rubbed her chin in thought. "But it's doubtful Grace is connected to this third set of murders, *if* it's even related to the others at all. However, if we find something pointing to Rourke, that'd strongly suggest he's the key to whoever's doing this."

"And it was conveniently performed while my only alibi would've been a deceitful vampire who already betrayed me once. It's not likely I'll remember what I was doing twenty-three years ago when I wandered in front of baby Grace giving her nightmares for life." His tone had dropped to a harsh bitter rasp, as if the thought of cursing Grace to live in terror of him every day of her life ate at his very soul.

Demetrius shrugged. "Well, you're a bastard, but you're not a pointless murderer."

Rourke nodded like he agreed with both the bastard label and murderer observation. "There's a few hours before daylight. Are you up for checking out the scene, Grace?"

Chapter Six

She'd feared him her whole life? Rourke had never been to the crime scene and couldn't flash them. They recovered Grace's vehicle from the trailhead, and Rourke drove Grace there. Two birds, one stone. Grace's car found in the middle of nowhere raised too many questions, and he got decompression time before they dealt with another tragedy.

Demetrius had been right. He should've changed, but he couldn't explain the need to get to Grace's side. He'd been away from her long enough. Manka's scent hung on him and he detested it. Detested himself. Not for doing his job, but that he'd further upset Grace after what she'd been through.

When he'd caught Grace sobbing in the bedroom, the urge to embrace her had won over.

Until she had declared he reeked.

He should've changed. Hellfire. Was that guilt? Another emotion wormed its way under his armor.

How the fuck could she have formed a memory of him, one of that horrible nature?

"I could've driven my own car." Grace's fingers tapped on the passenger door, her pink lips pursed.

"Demetrius gave me the address."

"You have a control issue, you know that?"

"Yes."

"Mm-hmm." Grace ceased the tapping only to use her fingers to check off statements. "You can't stand touching. You prefer women tied up so you can unlock them. I'm guessing so you can also fuck them with as little contact as possible." She raised an eyebrow in question.

He clenched his jaw and nodded. He owed her somewhat of an explanation, so he allowed her to continue dismantling his habits.

"You own hardly any possessions. What you do own isn't designed for comfort." Except his bed. "And your color base is black."

He gave one slow nod to confirm her observations.

"What happened?"

Compassion radiated from her. If it had been anyone else, he'd have handed the keys over and flashed across town. With Grace, his level of worthlessness stayed low.

He didn't answer. He couldn't. All he'd told Demetrius after they bonded over their bar brawl was that his family was inferior degenerates who had destroyed themselves with their greed.

Demetrius assumed Rourke came from a prime family. It was possible he didn't care. He was a male who measured people by actions, one of the reasons he was the closest thing to a brother Rourke would ever claim. Because his own brother deserved a long walk in the sunlight.

Grace stared out the window. He'd remained silent so long, she'd given up. It worked for him. If she pressed any longer, he had the disturbing sensation he'd spill every morbid detail.

Then she'd know he was just as ugly as the vampire of her nightmares.

"Here it is." He parked next to the black Denali belonging to the Guardians.

A tall, lanky shifter named Chayton met him outside. His shifter's golden eyes were grim. "Another one called in similar to last night. An anonymous tip I'm starting to think is from the killer."

Rourke's gaze roamed the place. Grace stood close to his side. He resisted stepping in front of her. She needed no protecting from the male. It was for Chayton's own protection because if he didn't stop his flagrant appraisal of her body, Rourke was going to play he-loves-me-he-loves-me-not with his limbs.

Chayton's nostrils flared, catching a whiff of Rourke's possessive instincts. The corner of his mouth lifted in a smirk, and he aimed his disgustingly handsome face toward Grace and extended his hand.

"Chayton. And you are?"

She dropped her fingertips into his clasp for a quick shake before yanking them away. Smart girl.

"Grace."

"The name suits you."

She blinked, taken aback. A pink blush stained her cheeks. Did Chayton embarrass her? Rourke would rip his tongue out and stomp on it. Wait, she wasn't offended. She liked the compliment. They weren't his strong suit and he often had no reason to give them. Not until Grace.

Smugness filled Chayton's expression. He was a fire starter, that one. If Rourke had sensed any true intentions behind the male's flirty words, he'd be dog meat by now.

"Give us the report, Guardian."

"She going in with us?" Chayton asked, inferring Rourke had gone mad.

"Yes, she is," Grace answered, throwing some attitude at Chayton.

Rourke may have gloated a little. "You heard the lady. Lead the way."

Chayton spun and entered the house. Death and blood assaulted Rourke. Grace covered her nose and mouth until she got used to it. Unfortunately, one *did* get used to it.

The Guardian pointed out bodies, listing evidence, similar to the night before. "The male and female vampire who own the house were murdered in their beds. The male died right away via beheading, but it appears the female was initially injured and fought back. Her body is at the bottom of the stairs. Her head is at the top."

Grace shook her head in disgust.

"We called you as soon as we walked in and smelled the sulfur taint. I scented more than one attacker," Chayton continued. "I also detected a third family member whose body we've been unable to locate." His expression turned grim. "A child. We found his room. Nothing seemed out of place."

Rourke's gut clenched at the news. He raised his nose, drawing in a deep breath, filing every detail away. "Same killers."

"I suspect so as well. Unless you need me, a domestic was called in and I love beating some abuser ass."

Rourke's opinion of Chayton climbed a few notches.

After the shifter left, Rourke walked the rooms slowly. Grace's gaze on his back burned a metaphoric hole in between his shoulder blades.

"What is it?"

"Is it déjà vu if it happens a *third* time?"

His head jerked up. Of course, what he was doing matched her nightmares of him. Perhaps, she shouldn't have come.

"Only—" She held her hand up. "No, don't move. Yeah, stand just like that." Her head tilted and turned, inspecting him. "The clothing's different obviously, although you—he—wore dark garments then, too." She continued to study him.

He'd remain a statue for eternity if that's what she needed.

Hellfire. Was he going to grow ovaries, too? This emotional rollercoaster around her and drive to please her…it wasn't right. It wasn't fair. He'd went through hell to become a cold, unfeeling prick.

She squatted down and narrowed her focus back on him.

Ah, she was trying to view the same angle as when she was a toddler.

"Something's different. I thought that last night, too. Something about my nightmare guy was crueler, harsher. You walk through here and your face is introspective. You're soaking in smells, observations, cataloguing everything. He was…he relished the violence."

"But you saw me."

"Yeah." She rose, uncurling her enthralling body wrapped a sweatshirt and jeans. "You don't have a twin running around do you."

Her tone was joking, but her words filled him with long-held rage.

It couldn't be.

"Rourke?"

That bastard. It made too perfect of sense. Grace couldn't have fabricated a dream of him when she'd only met him last night. But she could have encountered one who *resembled* him.

"Rourke? What'd I say? Seriously, do you have twin?"

He worked his jaw. He never spoke of his brother. If he didn't talk about him or utter his name, he didn't exist.

He and his people were behind this, just like they were behind every horrible thing that'd ever happened to him. Only now they'd targeted someone he…what? Cared about? He didn't know Grace well enough to claim that. Was invested in? That was it. His duty was to help her seek justice, only he'd be the one doling it out.

"Rourke?"

He blinked back into focus and renewed his investigation. "I need to search for evidence."

"What's going through that tortured mind of yours?"

He brushed off her question. Until he had proof, he wasn't telling anyone his suspicions. And when he did have proof, well…coming clean to Grace he was fucking responsible for her family's death didn't hit the top of his must do list.

He should've killed his brother when he had the chance.

"Dammit, Rourke. What is it?"

He schooled his features to his standard calm. "Nothing, Grace. I was processing all the clues. We're wasting night."

The fight faded from her as she let it go. He watched in amazement as the spark lit right back up. "Oh, God. There's a missing kid."

Rourke could only guess what his brother planned to do with a kid. "Go to the child's room, find out as much information as you can while I look into the murders."

Grace gingerly stepped around the gore and hit the stairs running. He lost precious seconds watching her curves bound up the stairs.

Back to work.

The house was small, well cared for, but rundown suggesting money was tight and had been for a while. Definitely not a prime family, but then snatching one of their children would be more difficult.

The child. If Rourke's brother had a hand in the abduction, his intention may be to sell the kid as a blood slave. Rourke clenched and unclenched his fists. Is that what he'd planned to do with Grace when he hunted her as a toddler?

Or, since the stench of brimstone hung in the air, had he advanced to more complicated deals? Selling kids to bond to demons the way Calli had been unwittingly forced to do?

How many children had they missed over the years?

But Grace's human family had no small children.

None of this made sense. He and Grace were tied to both of her family's murders, but not to this one. Demons were linked to all three. Rourke's brother was a possible suspect in the killings twenty-three years ago, and someone tried to frame Rourke for last night's murder.

Or send him a message.

One that said, *I'm not done with you yet, boy*. Words his father had said all those years ago when—Rourke couldn't remember the details. Just those words before he was sold.

He crouched down to inspect the mom's body. Deep gouges marred her flesh. Her head had been brutally severed. On impulse, he turned her body over. There on her back, drawn in her blood was a jagged "R."

As if he'd turned into a murderer and was stupid enough to sign his name. All serial killers had their tell, but it wasn't random clues pointing to one person. To him.

Rourke climbed the stairs. As he neared the parents' bedroom, a sense of foreboding crept into his gut. Entering the bedroom, he exhaled slowly and surveyed the scene. It matched what Chayton had described. The coward had taken the father by surprise, beheading him before he even woke. But it'd been enough to rouse the mom who fought wildly and lost.

A closed door at the edge of the room taunted him. Chayton may not have inspected it if he hadn't sensed anything inside. Rourke crept over, one foot in front of the other. He couldn't stop if he tried. Something waited for him behind the door.

He swung it open and waited. At first he picked up nothing. It was an empty bathroom. Flaring his nostrils, he smelled the dad's blood. Where it had faded toward the door, he was hit with a powerful shot as he stepped inside.

Scrawled in blood across the mirror was only one word.

Ozias.

It transfixed him, that one word. A confirmation of his suspicions. His past coming back to claim him. He sensed Grace approaching, but couldn't tear his gaze off those five letters.

"Ozias. What's that mean?" she asked, coming to a stop next to him. Side by side, their reflections stared back at them from the mirror.

"It's my name."

***

With dawn approaching, Grace couldn't waste time. She pulled a pale Rourke from the bathroom, down the stairs and out the door. Then she flashed them back to the car. As they drove to headquarters, she filled him in on the kid, a boy, not much older than she'd been. His name was Ari and she'd grabbed a few of his things: a teddy bear, a blanket, some clothes, and two cardboard books.

When Rourke had interacted, it was only to give her directions and gesture to the garage. She pulled in and killed the engine. Both Demetrius and the other male she'd met, Bishop, waited for them when they arrived.

"What'd you find?" Demetrius asked as Rourke.

"They're not framing me. They're sending me a message."

"Who?" Bishop asked.

"My brother, and whoever he's working for."

Grace and the other two males stared at Rourke. So she wasn't the only one surprised.

"I thought any family of yours were dead." Demetrius spoke what must've been on Bishop's mind because he nodded in shock.

"My mother and father are. I left them to perish for their own decisions. My brother disappeared, and I wasn't going to go looking for him. He was just as selfishly entitled as our parents." Rourke sank back against the car. "I should've ended him, too. Should've expected he'd make others suffer for his gain."

Grace stepped closer, in case he needed the support. He obviously did, but would he accept it?

"Why?" Bishop lifted a hand to lay on Rourke's shoulder, but pulled back. "We assumed you hated them, but why?"

A deep red filled Rourke's coffee brown eyes. When he spoke, his voice was hard, his words clipped. "They sold me as a blood slave."

Sheltered from their world, she could only guess what the term meant. Slavery would explain his reaction to her fang scraping him. His past was the foundation upon which Rourke had built his internal protections.

"Shiiit," Demetrius breathed. "I didn't know. I'm sorry."

Rourke slashed his hand through the air. "It's my baggage. It should not affect you. Any of you.

When I escaped, I killed the men who used me. It's over. Done."

Selling a child was atrocious. Diabolical. Heartless. The children Grace tutored were the definition of innocence. How could anyone extinguish the natural brightness of a child?

"Why did they do that to you?" Bishop's appalled tone expressed what they all felt.

Rourke sneered. "Claimed it was all I was good for anymore."

"Anymore?" Bishop questioned.

Rourke shrugged. "My life was just as shit at home as it was when I was captive." He inclined his head toward Grace. "I believe it's my brother she remembers. I remember a boy with lanky black hair who thought the world owed him everything. If he cleaned himself up, I'm sure we'd resemble each other."

He couldn't have told her at the house? Her heart broke for the brutalized boy he'd been, but as a man, he was frustrating as hell.

"We find your brother, we find answers." Demetrius considered Rourke. "You good?"

"Not until we find my brother and save the kid."

The trepidation for the boy was written across his features as clearly as his name had been scrawled across the mirror.

Which brought up another question: Why hadn't he told them about the blood messages?

"Finding the child is paramount," Demetrius agreed. "It's morning. The kidnappers are as stuck as we are. We'll resume in the evening." He pinned Rourke with a hard look. "You'll keep me updated on everything, Rourke. Take Grace, and I want Bishop working with you."

Rourke briefly tensed next to her as if insulted by the insinuation he needed assistance. Bishop's mouth pulled tight. They worked well together the previous night, Grace wondered what had changed.

Demetrius's gaze danced back and forth between the two, also sensing something off. "Keep them in line Grace." He handed her a card key. "Your room is ready. Rourke will show you the way. Your belongings are already inside." He strode out of the garage bay, Bishop on his heels.

Fatigue caught up with her. If Rourke hadn't been put through the emotional ringer in the last hour, she'd pepper him with questions. Not that he'd answer. After some rest, he'd probably reinforce his internal walls and it'd be impossible to pry any information from him.

"I'll show you to your room." He didn't sound defeated, but like he'd lost round one.

She shoved her car keys into her pocket and trailed him. Her familiarity with the building didn't extend to this portion. He stopped in front of a door nowhere near his apartment. She was tempted to grab her stuff and request to go back to his place. But there was no reason for her to stay with him. The attraction may be a one-sided deal.

Their kiss seemed to be ages ago between two different people. Before they were embroiled in a scheme where the players and their motives were unknown.

She held the card key against the reader and pushed the door open. Rourke's distracted gaze rested on the floor. He made no move to leave.

Delicious scents teased her. "Smells like they loaded me up with dinner. Why don't you come in and eat?"

"I should eat." His tone was flat, like he was just stating a fact.

"Yes, you should."

Ushering him into the room, she followed him inside. Her duffle and computer bag were settled inside by the door. Food and a shower sounded heavenly. She busied herself digging into the covered dishes Betty had left behind. From the herb-laced scents filling the suite, Betty was one hell of a cook.

Two leather chairs sat across from a television in the small sitting area outside the bedroom. He chose one to sit in. Grace prepared a plate of ribbon steak and seasoned potatoes for them both. Although the tiny kitchenette had a table with two chairs, she carried their food out and handed him his plate.

She set hers down and went in search of something to drink. Betty was on top of that as well. Water, soda, beer, and two bottles of wine stocked the shelves and counters.

A vice squeezed around her chest and she fought to breathe. She'd met Betty once; she met these vampires less than two days ago. Yet, they cared for her, welcomed her in, and accepted her as part of the investigation crew.

"What's wrong?" More life lifted Rourke's voice than she'd heard all night.

She almost answered with nothing, but there'd been enough nondisclosure for the night. "I'm just incredibly grateful to have a place to stay right now, and it's more than I could've asked for."

"Demetrius is like that."

With two wine glasses and an open bottle of red, she strode over so they could dig in. "How'd you meet him?" She didn't expect an answer.

Rourke precisely cut his meat and measured a forkful. She shoveled in a heaping mouthful, too hungry to take her time.

"Bar fight," he answered. "After I was free, I had nowhere to go. I fed off unsuspecting humans in alleyways like the vampires in B-movies. What money I stole, I drank away in a bar until it was time to stumble into some abandoned building to pass out during the day."

He swirled his glass of wine, studying it. "Betty seems to know what I drink. Anyway, Demetrius came in one day. I hated him on principle. Rich. Arrogant. Laughed too much."

Grace's lips twitched. That would've pissed Rourke off.

"After I drank the rest of my money, I challenged him. We went at it until we got kicked out, then we brawled outside. We were both drunk so it was a draw. As we were choking each other, I gritted out how I hated how our world worked. Prime families monopolize all the resources, pit the commoners against each other for work until they turn into the monsters humans fear. I hated us all. Prime, commoners, shifters, even humans."

He still did. Bitterness tainted his words that wasn't related to the retelling of his story.

"The fucker started laughing. He released me and asked what I wanted to do about it. The way he said it. The crafty bastard was already planning something. Whatever he was up to, I wanted in. He brought me in with the whole team. Bishop, Creed, Zoey, and Ophelia all went to prep school with him. They heard things about corruption in our government, started checking on them, and secretly began laying the groundwork for their big coup."

"He mentioned that."

His eyebrows shot up. "I forget you missed all that." He scowled into his wineglass. "Consider yourself fortunate. Basically the organization your parents worked for was run by our vampire government. Our team infiltrated them, turned them over, and buried them. That's the short version, anyway."

Grace placed her plate on the end table. She had one major question, and it'd either end the night or open up an avenue for conversation. "Your name is Ozias Rourke? Why didn't you tell Demetrius about the messages at the scene?"

Rourke's jaw clenched. His fork warped under his grip. "No one knew my full name until tonight. I let Demetrius assume Rourke was my first name. I let them all assume I'm from a prime family."

"Are you sure they don't know?"

He scoffed. "I respect Demetrius more than any male I've ever met, but do you see a plethora of commoners surrounding him? I wouldn't have been allowed into his inner circle if he knew I was just a Rourke."

So certain. She switched conversation topics. There had to be a ray of not-depressing light somewhere in his past. "Do you remember anything *good* from your childhood."

"Nothing before I was sold for my blood and body. Nothing afterward obviously."

She guarded her expression. Of course blood slave meant he was supplied for more than food. "Why would they do something like that?"

His attention caught the curvature of the fork. He hastily dropped it on his plate and stood, picking up her dishes, too. "My kin were swindling, sleazy people who cheated their way through life. They could make a buck off me, so they did."

His back remained toward her while he cleaned up the remnants of their meal. It was a metaphor for the wall he just reinforced between them. End of conversation.

"I'm going to shower," she announced. Gathering her duffel bag and backpack, she left her laptop bag rest where it was.

Going through the motions of cleaning herself, her mind pinged from the events since she'd left for a hike to her next lesson plan for the kids. Her life didn't need to be completely ruined. She could save her job, and she would need the money. She had nothing now except the charity of this group. She would have to keep her job. Wait, Grace Otto was done and gone. She had a solid reputation with the kids she tutored, but it was best for all of them if she resigned. But she could find a new online tutoring program—there were always openings. She could get a little sleep, beg Betty for Wi-Fi access, fill out a few applications, and upload.

Kids. Please let Ari be all right. Daylight imprisoned all vampires. She just hoped it did the same for his captors, that nothing more horrible than what Ari had already been through would happen. If only he'd been abducted by loving adoptive parents, but that situation was a bit like lightening striking in the same place twice.

Silence hung over the room when she stepped out of the bathroom. No big surprise Rourke cut and run. That he stayed for dinner reflected the inner turmoil he faced.

She was tired, but not cozy into sleep tired. Perhaps she could concentrate enough to record a lesson. Padding out into the sitting area, she pulled up short.

Asleep in the chair, slumped back, was Rourke. His head rested on the top of the seat, legs stretched out and crossed. Seizing a moment to study his features, her eyes roamed his face.

His patrician features were revealed when the hardness of his angles softened in slumber. Arching brows, a strong, straight nose and lips that had touched hers in wonder last night. The charcoal color of his clothing highlighted the olive tone of his skin.

The slope of his body as he reclined enraptured her. His slacks draped over prominent thigh muscles, the sweater rested on his hard stomach and was drawn across his chiseled chest. He was a beautiful male specimen. So unlike the humans she'd dated. Virile, dangerous, and with more layers than he let anyone glimpse. Sinful eyes and full lips that'd make an angel fall.

Isn't that what he'd called her in the woods?

A furrow creased his brow. His mouth pulled down in a frown. A second later, his features smoothed.

Nightmares for everyone, she mused.

Tiptoeing, she bent to retrieve her laptop.

A whoosh of air precluded Grace being lifted and pressed against the wall. Six-feet-three inches of seething vampire secured her at the throat and waist. The faraway glaze in his eyes was like a camera rolling through bad memories.

"Rourke," she rasped, "wake up." Her lungs were running out of air. If he didn't let up, she'd pass out and be at the mercy of a vampire reliving a nightmare.

Menace tightened his grip, his fangs bared, and oh…like the rest of him they were huge. Used for pleasure, it'd be an ecstatic experience. Used for violence, deadly.

She released the wrist he held at her throat and caressed his face. He propelled backward, and she slammed to the floor, gasping for breath.

"Grace?" Fully awake, horror flushed his expression. "*Oh shit*, did I hurt you?"

He dropped to his knees and with a gentle touch, lifted her to him. Her breathing eased, her initial distress diminished, and she clung to him. He pulled her close.

Her lips touched his neck with a soft kiss of invitation. He groaned, easing his mouth down to hers.

She met him with reserve. This time it was going to last. She rested her hands on his shoulders, prepared for him to bolt any second. He shivered under her fingers. Encouraged, she swept them along his torso. Fiery heat seeped through his soft sweater. He opened his mouth to delve into hers.

Grace's insides fluttered when his hands swept under her nightshirt. They might actually go further than a kiss.

Yesss.

His smoky, rich flavor made her want to plant a row of hickory trees just for burning, so she could replicate his scent when he wasn't around. But nothing could match the experience of Rourke.

As their tongues twined, Grace protected her fangs as much as possible. Nothing was going to come between them today. Heat built until she held a raging inferno within her core that screamed for the male to satisfy her. It stole her breath having never known lust this strong. When was the last time she'd been this turned on?

She been around good-looking men before. And while none of them possessed Rourke's exotic features and intensely coiled personality… No, no one compared. That was her answer to why the male affected her so.

He leaned her back, strong arms encircling her in a protective embrace until her back hit the floor. He hovered over her, pushing her pants down and her shirt up, while he was still connected to her via their kiss.

When he broke away, she gasped for air. His hands on her bare skin short-circuited her brain, making her forget things like breathing and heartbeat. It was all non-essential beyond his touch.

His lips fastened around a breast, and, oh god…can a girl come from that?

When his fingers slid down her sex to separate her, she moaned. Her eyelids drifted shut, but she snapped them open again to watch him lick a circle around her nipple. Then his fingers separated her until his thumb found her clit.

Burying her hands in his hair, she lost herself to his caress.

She met each stroke, rocking her hips, bringing her closer to an impending explosion, one that promised to be stronger than any in her past.

What past? It all felt like amateur games before this moment on the floor with her damaged vampire who touched her so intimately. Who allowed her touch. Who remained completely oblivious to the twisting of his hair. The thrill that her body absorbed his attention, dragging him away from his phobias was more intoxicating than any liquor around her parent's fire pit.

When he pushed a finger inside, a hoarse cry ripped from Grace's throat. She hitched her knees up, straining for his thrusts.

With a growl, he removed his hand leaving her bereft for two seconds before his tongue replaced it.

Her hands dropped from his hair to claw at the floor. If she'd thought his hand was on fire, his tongue virtually sent up steam tendrils.

Powerful hands gripped under her ass, pulling her closer.

The climax hit hard and fast. Grace cried her ecstasy until she felt sharp fangs strike her thigh. Air sucked into her lungs cutting off her cry. Pleasure swamped her until she knew nothing but the quakes of orgasm and fierce pulls on her vein, the combination blowing her ever-loving mind.

As he withdrew, she shuddered at the gentle swipe of his tongue.

She needed him inside of her. Sitting up, she tugged at his sweater.

Shock registered on his face, and he clambered back. "I still stink of the club." He removed the sweater and shredded it, his muscles bunching with each tear.

She reached for him, unabashed at her nudity. "Rourke. That sweater must've cost a fortune."

The stench of Manka was not a concern. She believed Rourke hadn't fucked her. His hesitance during their intimacy wasn't an act. Physical touch was not a daily occurrence for the male.

"I'm not a poor street rat anymore." He deposited the remnants in the garbage and turned to face her. "What is it about you, Grace?" His tone wasn't insulting, it wasn't passionate. He'd returned to his emotionless state. Or so he wanted to fool himself. "You make me want things better left alone."

"Why?" she challenged. "We both want each other. We're both adults."

"No, angel. You're a good person. You deserve a good life. I live to hunt scum." He made a disgusted noise, his hands dropping to his hips. "I can't be weakened by emotions. And when you find your true mate, you don't need me as baggage."

"Emotions don't make us weak." While she paled in comparison to him physically, her inner being had been nurtured and formed into a strong female.

"I need to control myself." He gestured to his manhood. "Look at what you do to me. I don't get hard. Not until a female is secured with her legs spread, her labia separated, and *only then* do I fuck her."

Grace's brows shot up at the description. And her body thrummed, even after what they'd done. "I'm sure it wasn't always that way." From the way his jaw worked, she nailed it. "The more time that passes, the more control you think you need, the more phobic you become about others."

"You don't know anything." His half-hearted statement fell flat between them.

Bull. Shit.

At her dubious expression, he spun toward the door. "I'm going back to my place."

She let him.

Chapter Seven

Rourke stared at his ceiling. Hands folded across his stomach and an erection that wouldn't fade resting on his hipbone.

What a shitty day.

He hadn't slept, tried to mediate and failed. Something tugged at his consciousness. It had to do with Grace, but it didn't. The weirdest thing he couldn't fucking explain.

He'd come back, cleaned Manka and the sex room's stench from himself, trashed his pants, and lay on his safe haven—his bed. As the rays of sunset faded in the sky, his body told him it was time to hunt.

He reached across his bed and dialed Bishop.

"I need you to watch over Grace and look for the missing kid. I'm hunting my brother. Alone."

"Those weren't Demetrius's orders."

"No. They weren't."

Bishop paused. He was going to cave. Rourke discerned him well. Bishop's reaction to Demetrius's command had unsettled him and it was personal. His partner had been distracted the past few weeks. Another curse to pile on Rourke's family—he was too damn busy dealing with his own drama to be of service to Bishop.

"I will inform him," Bishop said. "You have twenty minutes."

Rourke swung his legs down. Time to leather up, strap on his weapons, and reunite with his big brother.

***

Grace stuck close to the massive vampire. They were in a questionable part of Freemont she never realized existed. Disguised as a dive on the outside but a swanky country club on the inside, the environment was completely foreign to her. Expensive labels, painted faces, and gelled hair, and the activities… Grace watched premium cable, she'd seen some risqué things—on TV. But the sexual activities, just what was done in the public areas, far surpassed her imagination. The stench of sex seeped into the furniture, the walls, the floor. When she left, she was going to smell as bad as Rourke had.

Why did all of her musings land on that frustrating male?

"Our best shot at a lead on the kid is in this place," Bishop murmured to her, his tone apologetic.

"I'm a bit out of place." A zebra print headband contained her wild curls. A long-sleeved athletic tee paired with a fresh pair of jeans…she might as well be dressed in fluorescent from head to toe.

He glanced down in surprise. Typical dude, it hadn't occurred to him. "I think we can use it to our advantage. Play along."

His meaty fist wrapped around her arm and he dragged her behind him.

"Hey!"

They earned a fair share of swiveled heads.

"Bishop," a throaty voice purred, "you know we don't like commoners among our ranks." An Elvira worshipper slunk up to them and tilted her head, studying Grace.

Bishop tugged Grace closer as if protecting her from the old-world, elegant vamp.

Grace blatantly eyed the female in return. Her first thought was she didn't like this world. The dismal second thought reminded her it was her world now. No more middle class America where she worked behind a screen and flitted through the human world after dark blending in. But then in her opinion, class wasn't born, something this female didn't understand.

"She smells like him. Do you two share now?" She nodded knowingly. "Of course he shares. I should know. No wonder you had to bring her here. His favorite room is in the back."

Just like Grace didn't share her work laptop with anyone, she wasn't sharing her body. Play along, she reminded herself.

"Yes," Bishop replied. "He'll be here shortly. I'll make my way back to secure her, but I need a drink first."

Her husky chuckle was partly sinister, partly fond of Bishop. Her fingers drifted over the expanse of his shoulder. "You will learn to enjoy it. I never understood why you don't have the stomach for the play. A vampire's strength is wasted on the human women you frequent."

"I'm not picky. They're just plentiful."

Grace wanted to choke on her own vomit. Why did the thought of Bishop getting down and dirty make her feel like she'd interrupted Nathaniel after a too long shower?

"Oh, look at the poor commoner," the Elvira vampire purred. "We're scaring her. When Rourke's done with her, I'll finish him off the right way."

"Get your sense of smell in line," Grace snapped. "It's disgust. Guess this *commoner's* senses are more refined."

The female bared her fangs, lunging for Grace. Bishop stopped her with a hand at her chest.

"Leave it. She's a free vampire, and she responded to your insult. Nothing more."

Elvira ran her tongue down her fang. It was supposed to be menacing.

Grace squinted at her teeth. "Do you have a piece of steak stuck in your teeth? What's with your tongue?"

Bishop coughed a laugh. The female's eyes flared wide. She hissed at Grace, flung a final glare at Bishop, and stormed away.

"We were supposed to be discreet." Humor crinkled the corner of Bishop's eyes.

"I'm sorry. I'm not a worldly vampire trained in the art of being a condescending bitch." And the comment of bedding Rourke made her own fangs ache to bury themselves in Elvira's throat.

"Well, I don't think we'll find out much here. Not after that reception." Bishop urged her to leave, when a bark stalled them.

"Where is he?" Three males, all shorter than Bishop, but much, much taller than Grace flanked them.

The exit door at Grace's back became extremely inviting.

"I know I'm dumber than I look, you'll have to be more specific." Bishop crowded her behind him, creating a barrier between her and the wave of rage rolling off the males.

"The son of a bitch dusted Manka and left her scattered ashes for us to find."

Manka. The female Rourke stunk like because he'd been trying to get answers. The female who'd stolen from him to set him up for a crime she participated in—killing the three people Grace loved.

Grace felt no pity.

"It was official business." Bishop squared off against them. Grace couldn't even see the males beyond his broad back. "Manka committed a serious crime. She defied the Synod's mandates."

"That filthy animal won't be allowed to walk out of here if he ever enters again. We'll neuter him."

The muscles in Bishop's back went rigid at the insult and threat. "And they'll grow back, dumbass. Then he'll kill you."

Hisses reached her ears. "I think we need to send him a message."

The words were directed at Grace, and she knew exactly what they meant.

"Run, Grace." Bishop crouched and met the attackers head-on. She had zero fighting experience; she sprinted for the door.

An attempt at flashing yielded no success. Did they do something to the club or was it just her terror?

Yanked back into a hard chest, she twisted and dropped to the ground. Kicking out with her leg, she tripped the male who'd pinned her. A bellow from Bishop had him spinning to bury his meaty fist into the male.

Grace scrambled to her feet and raced for the door. Glancing over her shoulder, she saw Bishop's limbs swinging, punching, kicking. How could a giant be so graceful? Any guilt she had at deserting him drained away. She'd only be a liability, and it'd take two more vampires fighting against him to make it an even fight.

Out in the night, she ran in the direction of Bishop's Hummer. Her flight came to an abrupt stop when she slammed into a body that suddenly appeared.

Strong arms steadied her and for one second her mind almost sighed in relief at the smoky smell that greeted her.

But this scent was laced with brimstone.

Raising her eyes, she gazed into a pair much like Rourke's, only darker. Rourke's brother wore a sinister smile and pulled her closer.

"We meet again, Grace."

She opened her mouth to blast his eardrums with a shattering scream, but he laid a finger across her lips.

She snapped at it.

He only chuckled. "Don't make a scene. I wouldn't want anything to happen to your parents."

"They're dead." Her foot stomped down onto his, but he only winced slightly.

"What you don't know is they weren't your parents."

She stilled.

No lie came from him. Did the demon influence prevent the action?

His chest rumbled in a chuckle. "That's right. They were your babysitters. Your real parents are alive, and they think you're dead. But if you're really good, I'll tell you who they are."

Her decision was made. "I'll go with you."

Chapter Eight

The young boy peered up at Rourke.
He'd put the kid's age at around nine, but he could be older. Like humans, if not given enough nourishment during the formative years, vampires did not reach their full height potential.

Rourke's masters had wanted him strong. Once sold, Rourke finally experienced a moderately full belly.

Before that, his life paralleled the street urchin in front of him. Living in a rundown shack that should be condemned in a poor part of the city. Running the streets as a kid to scavenge anything from food to money to something that could be sold for food or money.

Cut off from the primes' resources, unable to secure employment with the wealthy families, commoners couldn't just go out and get a job as vampires. Some managed, but nightshifts weren't the most high-paying jobs around.

"I told ya, I don't know who lived here before us." The boy's eyes darted to the left and right.

Smart kid. Always plan a way out.

Rourke pulled a twenty from his pocket. The kid stepped in and Rourke took a long step back, sending him a warning look. "Keep your distance, boy. If my wallet disappears, I'll hunt you down and expect interest."

After a brief flare of alarm, the kid's expression turned shrewd. "Gimme the money and I'll find out…if you triple it."

"I don't just want their names. I want to know what happened to all of the Rourkes." He noticed the boy calculating the info, but Rourke beat him to the equation. "I'll pay you a hundred—on top of this." He waved the twenty.

Snatching the twenty, the kid took off with a, "Wait here."

Young humans wandered by. Some sizing him up, most ignoring him. He might get trouble from the stupid ones, but the majority of humans listened to their instincts that said he was a male that shouldn't be fucked with.

Rourke scanned up and down the street. Same buildings, more wear and tear. Shops were boarded up because no one could keep a business open for long. Too much theft, not enough law enforcement.

A half hour later, light steps smacking the pavement turned his head. The boy skidded to a stop an acceptable distance away and held a hand out.

"Not how this works," Rourke informed him. He pulled out the cash so the kid could see he was good for it.

A scowl lit his youthful face. "Look, I went to one of the old-timers. He said his pa talked of the Rourkes, how they disappeared like sixty years ago without paying their mortgage. The old-timer thought they had two kids, but one died when he was a little older than me."

Rourke bit his tongue to keep from baring his fangs. Died. He had wished many times.

"The other kid grew up and left home. Old guy said one night the Rourkes were just gone. He heard arguing 'n' shit and then they were gone. Left all their crap behind. After that, it's been a stream of various people. Want their names? I can give 'em to ya for an extra twenty."

Osiris was gone when their parents disappeared, but it didn't mean he didn't have anything to do with it. He was always an ambitious bastard. Rourke doubted he'd dulled in that area any.

"I don't need the names." Rourke passed the kid the hundred and withdrew another twenty. "Keep this one for yourself."

A small hand snatched them and pocketed the bills while he furtively glanced around. It wasn't necessary. Rourke ensured no one saw their transaction, otherwise he would've pinned a giant target on the kid.

Gritting his teeth in frustration, he strolled down the filthy street. Where the hell had Osiris slunk to? He'd left home and gotten involved with demons before traumatizing his Grace.

His Grace.

Her taste was seared into his being and her blood sang through his veins. He was pleasantly full for the first time in his life.

His steps slowed. Grace must be hungry. Would she feed while she was with Bishop? His lip curled into a snarl. Would she feed *from* Bishop?

A growl escaped. Grace's fangs touching any other male made him empathize with the shifters who go feral. Rage with no direction…unless he found the individual Grace had fed from, then it'd be destructive. Male, female, he didn't like it. He wanted Grace to feed from him.

Rourke experienced the customary recoil he usually did toward feeding. Only it wasn't as strong with Grace. Lust almost overpowered years of abuse.

His phone vibrated in his pocket. When he pulled it out, Bishop's name read across the screen.

As soon as he picked up, Bishop's rough voice cut through. "Is she with you?"

Rourke slowed to a stop, dread sinking into his bones. "If you're talking about Grace, you'd better be fucking with me."

Bishop swore. "I took her to Sharpe Pointe to get a lead on the boy, but I was jumped by three guys outraged about Manka."

"It was quick." Relatively. "They should be grateful."

"I told Grace to run, and now I can't find her."

Can't find her banged around his skull. "Did she flash back to her home? To the trail where her parents were killed? What about headquarters."

"I've never been to her home, but I'm driving there. I tried the woods where we were last night and headquarters."

Rourke didn't bother looking around to ensure there'd be no witnesses to his sudden disappearance. He flashed to Grace's home and busted inside. It was already partially empty thanks to the team Demetrius hired to remove the Ottos' stuff."

Any trace of her scent from the previous night had dissipated. She wasn't there.

"Don't bother with her home. She hasn't been here."

A loud thump resonated through the phone as Bishop hit the dash of his car. "There's a park down the street. Meet me there so we don't make the neighbors suspicious."

The scent of fresh blood hit his nostrils. He glanced down. The hand not holding the phone bled from where his nails dug into his skin. Forcibly, he unclenched his fist.

Calm. Controlled. He was not an animal.

But if Grace was harmed, he'd become a monster.

***

Grace jerked her elbow free from Osiris's grasp. He'd flashed her to a…holy moly, was that a mansion?

They stood in front of an ornate door. Polished wood arched high above her head. Osiris opened it and ushered her in.

She recalled Rourke flashing her to the entrance of his headquarters and how she couldn't flash in the club. It wasn't her. Some buildings must be no flashing zones and this was one of them.

Several smells assaulted her as she studied her surroundings. Old world elegance. Heavy embroidered fabrics hung off the walls, massive antique furniture dotted the room, and the shiny, black flooring had to be marble. Whoever built this place wanted everyone to know they were filthy rich. Was this how the prime families lived?

"Who are my parents?"

Osiris smiled down at her. She was struck by a face so similar to Rourke's *smiling*. God, he'd look handsome. But on his brother…she suppressed shudder. He was like a snake eyeballing lunch.

Sorry, she'd already fed her predator for the day. Ceasing those thoughts before arousal wafted off her, she tapped her foot with impatience.

"We need to discuss the terms of our deal first, Grace. Come."

Following Osiris was like getting invited to tea by a serial killer. Which, if there was tea, was

~127~

exactly what was happening. Other than the brimstone, his scent didn't match what she'd smelled in the woods. It was a little familiar from the crime scene the previous night. Even if he didn't strike the death blows, he was involved in all of them, she was sure of it.

He led her into a large office with floor to ceiling windows—a bold move for a vampire. An ornate desk sat in front of the windows. He took a seat behind the desk and gestured to an obnoxious high-back chair.

"This place yours?"

He inclined his head. Moonlight glimmered across his hair. Again her mind conjured Rourke in the woods when they'd met. She needed to distract herself.

"What a dive."

A grin spread across his face. Unlike his brother, he easily showed emotion, but it wasn't genuine. At least with Rourke, there was no pretense.

"We need your help." He reclined back and steepled his fingers while his calculated gaze rested on her.

As if. "Oh?"

"I'm afraid my brother's gotten out of control." He paused for dramatic effect. "He killed your human parents."

Grace's brows shot up. Osiris didn't know she remembered him. "How do you know?"

"We've been tracking him. Settled in Demetrius's crew, he's nearly untouchable. He attacked your caregivers, then the humans who raised you. If I were to guess, I'd think he has an obsession with you."

"But he didn't kill the family from last night."

Surprise flitted across his face. "There were more murders?"

He was good. Grace couldn't tell if he was full of shit or not. Osiris sat forward, his expression grave.

"Can someone account for Ozias's whereabouts?"

"I guess he was with," Grace wanted to gag on the words even knowing nothing happened, "another woman."

"Human?"

Grace shook her head.

His scrutiny gave her shivers, but she kept her breathing steady. Something was going on in the vampire world. She was involved. Rourke was involved. And Osiris was most definitely involved. Her human upbringing didn't have many advantages in the game, but she had unique access to most of the players. She'd use that.

"A vampire with Rourke's strength wouldn't need much time to decimate—how many victims?"

"Hopefully only two, maybe three. There's a boy missing." *Which you well know.* Grace wanted to find that little boy before he suffered the fate that had been waiting for her all those years ago.

"Indeed?" Osiris's words oozed with deceit. "Even with three victims, Ozias is an experienced killer. Can the female account for every minute?" His voice dripped with suspicion.

Bile crept up her throat. It's hard to be an alibi after death. Grace despised how Rourke's character was dependent on him being with Manka. If he'd been strapping down a male, would she still have issues?

Probably not. Just the idea of Rourke with another female filled her with seething rage. He'd said Zoey struck the killing blow, but Rourke didn't have a history with her as far as Grace knew.

"Grace. Were there any clues that pointed to Rourke?"

Like he was stupid enough to sign his name? How to get around the question without lying enough for him to smell it.

"Demetrius didn't mention any." It was hard to when he wasn't there.

"He wouldn't." Disgust dripped off Osiris's tone. "He's protected Ozias for decades. You can help, Grace."

"Rourke's searching for the boy, though."

Did Grace imagine his left eye twitch? He hated being reminded about Ari. Did that mean the boy was alive or dead?

His expression betrayed nothing. "It's easy to lead the search astray when you know where the missing person is."

He was alive? "And when do you tell me about my parents? Before or after I help?"

His eyes briefly darkened to full black.

Grace didn't know what caused it, but her intuition screamed it was wrong and the spike in brimstone was a strong hint of evil.

"My brother could kill others, even your real parents. Do you not want to put a stop to him?"

"I have only you to believe, and we just met. Perhaps if I met them…" *Please, please, please don't be messing with me.*

If her birth parents were still alive…Grace's hopes soared. They'd be strangers—would they recognize her? If they did, would they accept her? But she had no one else. Had repeatedly lost her loved ones—or she had thought. Parents who were alive…The idea filled the gaping chasm torn open within her two nights ago.

The atmosphere within the room had grown colder, even while Grace sweated under her collar. The stench of sulfur swelled and seeped away until a bare taste lingered.

Osiris studied her. She twiddled her fingers in her lap. It was an appropriate time to let her nerves shine.

"You have two nights to gather information, Grace."

"Three days grace is more common." Jokes about rock bands fell flat on Osiris. Damn her mouth. Like her mom accused, *No filter, Grace. You have no filter.*

"Two. Nights. Tell no one, not about me, not about your parents. No need to give my brother another target. Monitor Ozias's habits and report back to me."

And she was supposed to go off on her little errand not knowing if he spoke the truth. "Then do I get to their information?"

Osiris opened a side drawer in the desk and pulled out a photo. He slid it across the desk. "I'll give you your parents when you give me Ozias."

Grace's hand trembled as she tugged the picture toward her. She inhaled sharply when her eyes landed on the vampires in the picture.

If Osiris was lying, he found a couple who resembled her. The female's golden skin was several shades lighter than Grace's, while the male's skin tone reminded Grace of fine chocolate. Her own skin color fell smack in between, like her eye color.

As for hair, if this guy was her dad, she didn't know where her curls came from. He was bald as could be. The natural highlights were all from her mom. Grace was average height among humans, and she'd noticed, short compared to vampires. If she stood next to this couple, she'd be shorter than them both.

Perhaps Osiris lied. Her entire being screamed he didn't.

"You look like them," he commented.

"I do." She placed the picture back on the desk. There was no way she could keep their meeting secret if Rourke found the picture. And she wanted it kept secret, until she knew what was going on. "I'm sure I'm shorter than them, though."

"Not a surprise. Obviously the Otto's nourished you, but not like vampire parents could. If you had been reared by vampires, you'd be at least three inches taller."

Her human mom and dad had taken turns feeding her. But Osiris was correct. She'd suffered from mild blood hunger for years until she could hunt for herself. She'd never ingested vampire blood and it must be different.

With the thought of blood came a rumble from her belly.

"Are you hungry, Grace?" His voice dropped an octave and arousal rose from him like steam tendrils.

Starving.

He pushed up a sleeve. "May I offer?"

The sanguine color to his eyes told Grace he'd gladly do more than feed her.

Her stomach revolted. She put her hand to her mouth. "Thank you for the offer, but I'll have to pass."

His eyes narrowed on her, the red drained out. He held up his arm. "It's just from the wrist."

"I'm just—with all the excitement, my stomach's not feeling so hot."

"Indeed." A calculating gleam entered his eye. "Your parents for Rourke, then? I hate to add that, while I wouldn't want any harm to befall your family, again, it's dire we contain Rourke. If he finds out about them, I guarantee they'll be dead within hours. Maybe…he'll even lose it and kill the boy."

The threat was obvious enough. She had two nights and she only had to report on Rourke's routine. Two days to figure out what the hell to do. "My parents for Rourke." She left Ari out of it, like, maybe he'd forget his threat against the child. The couple in the picture, if they were who Osiris said, were at least adults.

He pinned her with a dark stare. "The carnival's in town. In two nights, meet me there by the Ferris wheel."

Odd choice for a vampire concerned with stately elegance.

Osiris rose and walked around the desk. "We'll go there now, so you'll know where to flash and where to meet me. The various smells will cover my scent on you. I trust you are intelligent enough to fabricate a story of your whereabouts?"

He assisted her to standing, which she hated. Withdrawing her arm from his grip, she backtracked until she was outside again. His hand slid around her arm once more, and he flashed them away.

Chapter Nine

Grace wandered through the carnival. It was winding down for the night, but humans strolled through for last minute games and rides.

She loved this place. So many good times. She and her mom riding all the fastest rides while her dad gazed on with a greenish tint to his skin. Nathaniel always competed against her, trying to win the biggest stuffed animal without having to fork over all the cash. She smiled at the memory, then it slowly faded.

Bishop had ensured she had her phone and programmed all of their numbers into it.

She didn't call anyone. Not yet. She didn't flash anywhere. Not yet.

Too much to sort through before she jumped into "the game" with both feet, playing both sides.

Screams of delightful terror surrounded her. She used to be one, lending her voice to the chorus of the rides. Brightly colored lights, spinning and flashing, brought a smile to her face. It was so utterly normal. The smell of fried dough teased her nose. Man, she could go for some cheese buttons.

Strolling through the games, she was propositioned by vendor after vendor. No money, no games. She had two nights to figure out how to apply for a job. Otherwise her no money situation would be long-term. She wouldn't be welcome at headquarters forever, and where would she go if Rourke found out she was working with his brother?

What was she going to do? Osiris's slick words didn't sway her belief in Rourke. He was not a heartless murderer.

Osiris had to be the one she remembered. She had no recollection of the killings, hadn't actually seen who'd struck the fatal blows.

Brother against brother. She was supposed to hand one to the other. Didn't matter who. Rourke would want Osiris's head if she told him what happened tonight. The only difference was he'd do it himself instead of using her as a pawn.

Learn Rourke's routine. Report to Osiris. She'd do that and figure out the rest. With Rourke's skills, that little bit wouldn't hurt him.

She was pulling up Bishop's number on her phone when she sensed a presence behind her.

An average looking man smiled at her like he was the best thing since high-speed internet. "Hey, there."

Her finger paused over the send button. Before her world tipped over, she'd take advantage of a situation like this. Get a human alone. Feed.

The guy was as appetizing as a week old funnel cake, but she couldn't pass him up. Even as her stomach twisted, she pocketed her phone and gave him a demure smile.

"Hey, yourself."

His eyes lit up thinking he'd found a bed companion. Or an against-the-wall buddy. "You here alone?"

"Not anymore. Want to walk me to my car?"

With an I-can't-believe-my-luck grin, he walked next to her and chatted. The parking lot was dotted with cars. There were plenty of streetlights, but they'd look like they were making out when she pinned him against whatever car she decided on to take a vein.

She led him to the far edge, behind the tallest pickup she could find. He crowded her into door.

"I can't believe a sexy thing like you was all by her lonesome," he murmured.

Enough small talk. She grasped his chin and caught his eyes. They glazed into the trance. She was free to feed and he wouldn't remember.

Licking her lips and eying his throat, she cocked his chin up to bare his neck. Her stomach roiled. If she'd eaten anything, this dude would be wearing it.

Strength was necessary for the upcoming days. She bared her fangs, leaned in, paused to gag, then struck.

Salty skin stung her tongue. Warm blood flooded her mouth. Another gag. She squeezed her eyes shut and persuaded herself to swallow.

As the blood was forced down her esophagus, more flooded into her mouth.

Her brain came on board with her body and she couldn't fight both of them.

Her fangs ripped out, tearing his skin. Trance broken, he barked out a cry. She doubled over, throwing up every drop of his blood.

Her victim staggered back against the vehicle. She sank to all fours and wretched on the ground, coughing and spitting, trying to get control over her rebelling body.

The man clapped his hand over his neck where red rivulets traveled down over his shirt. "What the fu—Did you bite me? Are you one of those freaky chicks who's into that shit?"

He scuffled away from her, but her higher thinking kicked in. She snagged his shoe and he tripped.

"No way, bitch." He kicked her hand loose. When he drew his leg back to stomp on her, she calculated the movement. As his foot flew toward her face, she wrapped her hand around his ankle and dragged him under her.

Realizing he was no match for her strength, his eyes widened with fright. Grace perched on top of him and held his face between her hands. Whether this would work or not, she had no experience.

Trancing him like she was going to feed, she spoke quickly.

"I tried to mug you, we got into a fight. Your nose bled." She released him and spit over her bite to heal it. The blood trail running down his neck hadn't dried. She rubbed her fingers around in it and smeared it over his nose and lip.

If her mental suggestion didn't work, he'd at least question his memories. For good measure, she tapped his nose. He groaned and his eyes rolled up into his head. To him, it probably felt like a full-fledged punch.

Grace crouched and scanned the lot. No witnesses that she could tell. Everyone drifting through were engrossed in their own nightly adventures.

The guy moaned. She flashed away.

Birds and crickets filled the night air. She found herself where it all had started, in the woods by the river, where her life had diverged from the isolated protection she'd grown up with.

She dropped against a tree trunk. Had she accosted a human? Now she was going to go back and be what, a double agent?

FML to the extreme.

No tears came tonight. Her sorrow was there, buried deep in her chest forever. Osiris hung her birth parents over her head, but her mom and dad were gone. Her best friend…she'd never get to laugh with Nathaniel again. But a switch had been flipped. Maybe she was in survival mode, maybe this was her heritage rearing its head.

Survival. Retribution. She wouldn't stop until she had answers. No—the truth. Her family deserved it. *She* deserved it, and she'd play the game to find out.

This time when she pulled up the contacts in her phone, it was Rourke she texted.

I'm where we met.

She held it, waiting for the vibration of his reply.

Leaves fluttered around her and a pair of black boots appeared at her feet.

Rourke crouched down. She raised her eyes.

Her heart stuttered and her blood hunger roared back.

What a male. Concern was buried deep in his dark gaze, eyes so much like his brother's. Except Rourke's irises had never flashed an eerie black.

"Where were you?" His voice was a low rumble, half accusing, half worried.

"Is Bishop okay?"

A hint of approval lightened his gaze to a rich brown. The question wasn't part of her act. She was genuinely fond of Bishop, and while he handled himself superbly against three able-bodied males, she wasn't a fighter. Things could've ended differently for all she knew.

"Frantic he lost you and it's his fault."

She sighed back against the tree trunk. "I'm fine. I'd rather he concentrate on finding Ari."

"He's on it." The heat of Rourke's gaze roamed over her. His mouth tightened, his expression turned murderous when he noted the blood around her face, on her hands, sprayed onto her shoes.

"Who do I have to kill?" His lip curled up, revealing a long white fang.

How messed up was it that his proprietary tone turned her on?

He has an obsession with you...

She didn't believe, couldn't believe, Rourke had entered her life just to destroy everyone she was close to. Even as he looked ready to commit atrocious crimes because of the blood covering her.

"No one. He was the victim." She scrubbed her face, but dried blood wasn't easy to get off. It'd have to wait for a shower. "The carnival's in town. I flashed there to escape, plenty of humans and all." Not a complete untruth. "I thought I should try to feed, but it didn't turn out well."

"How?" Rourke stood and stepped back. His brow creased and his mouth turned down, like her admission bothered him.

After his reaction to her fang scrape, she didn't think he'd offer to feed her. If it was a possibility, she'd have planted herself at his door in anticipation.

She panted, focusing on his neck and sinking her fangs into his flesh. Her hunger stirred into a frenzy.

"Grace, what happened?"

He was asking her questions. Closing her eyes to gather her control back, she inhaled deeply. "I puked up everything. He almost got away still bleeding from my fang marks. I think I took care of his memory, though, and sealed the wound. Made it look like he got a bloody nose from a fight we got into."

He nodded in approval. "Good thinking."

Of course her beating up a human didn't faze him. Not when she and Bishop were jumped at the club because his job was to coerce answers and to punish a female, one who helped commit an atrocious crime as a game.

He was everything Osiris painted him to be. Except he wasn't. He was his duty. His emotions were kept in check, encircled in a wall erected to protect a child left with no way out.

Rourke possessed the inner rage. The cold, calculating demeanor. It was all a part of him, but it was superficial as well. How the two brothers' pasts had diverged when Rourke was sold was the key. She wasn't a vampire shrink, but she doubted Osiris had experienced near the atrocities Rourke had. Unless he had and that's why he's much more dangerous.

"You need to feed." He said it simply, but his tone said he knew the answer to her hunger was him, and he didn't like it.

Well, that made two of them.

"It's been a few days. I should." She pushed herself up. Her time hiding in the woods was up, though she could stay here with Rourke all night. Considering the place, it made sense. It was like her family's presence lingered, faint but enough to comfort her. It was quiet, mimicked her life up until a couple nights ago.

"Perhaps Zoey or Ophelia will offer a vein." His lips flattened.

Her hunger mirrored his dismay. "I don't know. I'm still not feeling well. Is there a blood version of food poisoning?"

"Only when…" His frown was in full bloom.

"When what?" If she had some dread sickness, she wanted to know.

While he figured out what to say, she admired his broad shoulders in his tight, black shirt. He was just as hot clothed as he was with no shirt. Man, she wanted to see those abs again. All that smooth olive skin rippling over cut muscles. He didn't work out; he was just made that way. His waist tapered into leather pants fitted snugly over muscular thighs and incited all her girly fantasies.

The men she'd dated were pleasant enough in the looks department. Their bodies were like hers— okay. She wasn't the defined, shapely goddess Calli was, nor was she the willowy, strong females she spied at the club. When those males jumped Bishop, she'd been partially relieved because she hadn't been excited about her plain, frumpy body wandering among cover models.

"Vampires often have trouble feeding from others after they meet their true mate."

Her parents had taught her about mates, but not the specifics. She had equated mating with marriage in the supernatural world. What was he saying? She had trouble feeding from someone else because she's hot for Rourke?

"Do you know what true mates are, angel?"

The way her said her name. Like he stroked her center every time. "Boyfriend-girlfriend?"

"Much more. They recognize each other instantly and until the official mating ritual is performed, they can be with no others physically, though feeding abilities vary. Some reject other blood completely. Some just don't care for another vein. Do you…" He drifted off again as if he abhorred his next question. "Do you feel strongly drawn to Bishop?"

"No! He's like a giant teddy bear I feel safe around." Her uneasy gut improved at the thought of taking Rourke's vein. Could it be…mates? A thrill of excitement shot through her.

The side of his mouth twitched like he was dangerously close to a smile. "Teddy bear, indeed. What about any of the males at the club? Did any of them attract you in any way?"

Irritation quickly took over. After what they shared hours ago, he asked about other males? "In case my orgasm didn't clue you in Rourke, *you* may be the one I'm interested in."

His mouth tilted down again. For a dude who didn't emote, he sure frowned a lot. "It can't be. I don't feel it."

She reared back like she'd been slapped. "You didn't feel anything while I was orgasming against *your face*?"

"Lust of course. Vampires are sexual creatures."

What the—How could he just—Why was he being obtuse? "You yourself said you don't like to touch. Do you get that intimate with your former lovers?" She could've said *previous* lovers, but former felt much more accurate.

"Partners. None of them are lovers."

"And what was I? Partner or lover?"

"We did not fuck. You are neither." Cold Rourke had returned.

Asshole Rourke.

"You know what? I'm hungry, and there's a couple hours before sunrise. Obviously, we're not true mates so I have no feeding obstacles. I should hunt." She flashed to the parking lot where she'd parked those two nights ago to get away from Rourke and plan where she could lure in a meal.

It was the last thing she wanted to do, but it would get done. Out of spite!

His presence landed next to her. "You aren't going to hunt," he growled.

"Go home, Rourke. I'll return when I'm done." She couldn't flash to her old house.

It wasn't the best idea to pop into the place Osiris had shown her as being a generally safe area to flash, but the carnival was where she went. The fair had gone quiet, having closed for the night during her time in the woods.

A strong hand gripped her arm and she spun to face an irate pair of rich brown eyes.

"Why do you insist on following me, Rourke? Are you offering to feed me?"

He paused, his hand dropping from her arm.

"I thought so." She stormed through the steel monstrosities that sat quiet for the rest of the night.

His reaction to her shouldn't hurt her feelings. He and his partners could fuck around as much as they wanted, but Grace didn't unless she was invested in the relationship in some way. It'd only been two nights since she'd met Rourke, but he meant something to her. She didn't know what, but he was different.

He stalked her through the fair, the heat from his incensed body radiated to her. Her body reached for it like a drug.

"Grace, stop."

"Go home, Rourke. This isn't any of your business."

"You are my business." He reached out for her arm again.

For a dude who doesn't like to touch, his hands were on her a lot.

She spun on him to lay into him about everything pissing her off about him—from his insanely attractive face to his cologne-ad body to his shitty personality when faint footsteps reached her ears.

"Someone's coming." Instead of flashing away, because she didn't know where to go and she didn't want to return to her room in the middle of nowhere, she sprinted to the nearest ride promising the most cover.

She jumped the short fence surrounding the Tilt-a-Whirl and chose a seat where the high metal back provided cover. Sliding into the bench seat, she glanced over to find Rourke right next to her.

A human might have caused a ruckus running over the metal plates comprising the base of the contraption, and rocked the steel cup they sat in, but their vampire reflexes weren't as clunky. She was agile, and he moved like a ghost.

"Hello?" the voice of the security guard called.

Light from a flashlight bounced off railings and signs around them. Grace held her breath.

Rourke leaned over, his lips tantalizingly close to her ear. "Don't you dare consider him a meal."

It hadn't occurred to her. With his breath tickling the sensitive skin around her neck, she couldn't think of anything other than Rourke's lips.

The man's footsteps eventually receded.

"Then who do you suggest I feed from?" she hissed.

His eyes blazed, his lips flattened, and his hands curled into fists. "You want to feed so damn bad."

A gasp escaped her when he brought his wrist to his mouth and bit into it. The scent of his blood hit her and she was as entranced as the man she'd attacked earlier.

He pushed his wrist against her lips. A cold, impersonal way to feed, but to Grace, it was the sexist experience she'd ever had.

His rich, smoky blood filled her mouth. There was no urge to gag, her stomach purred in delight.

After several greedy pulls, her gaze flicked to Rourke and she stopped, drawing her tongue over the vicious wound.

The torn expression on his face broke her damn heart. Conflicted with desire and terror, it was obvious he fought back horrible memories.

"Oh god, Rourke. I'm so sorry." She returned his wrist to his lap, wishing she could replace his shell-shocked expression with something positive.

"Don't be. It felt good." His robotic tone didn't make her feel any better.

"Just because it felt good physically, doesn't mean it did your mind any good."

His met her gaze with surprise. "How do you know?"

"What?"

He gave his head a curt shake. "Nothing."

"It was clear you weren't enjoying it. Or you were, but it was giving you flashbacks." With terrible realization, she decoded what he'd asked. "Rourke, you were abused. Just because they manipulated your body into feeling pleasure doesn't mean you were okay with their actions. I'm guessing vampires can't help how feeding feels, pleasurable no matter what. It was wrong. Awful and wrong."

He exploded in movement. She tensed, prepared for his rage at her interference into his past. Instead, his mouth pressed down on hers, his hands tunneled under her sweater, then switched direction to drag down her pants. With a snarl of frustration, he tore her zipper apart to peel them down her legs and shove each shoe off. Somehow, they sustained their kiss. His tongue pushed inside, and she met it with enthusiasm.

Cool night air wafted over her bare legs while her butt pressed into the chilly seats. He wedged himself in between. Her hands gripped his shoulders for dear life. She didn't dare touch him in any other way because she didn't want him to stop. Since he'd arrived in the woods, her body had prepped itself for him.

Any time he was around, her body readied itself.

He broke away from her to undo the clasp of his leathers. When his shaft was freed, she had seconds to register his size and girth before he shoved her legs farther apart and placed himself at her entrance.

She was wet for him, but…he was a large male. Her fingers dug in to him and she tried to relax to accept him.

"I won't hurt you, Grace."

She pried her eyes off his manhood to meet his gaze. He'd acted as if he was out of his mind with lust, but he was fully present in the moment and concerned about her well-being. As if he hadn't dug into her heart with the quandary that was Rourke, he'd fully taken root.

Yes, he could prep her, loosen her up with his mouth, with his fingers, she didn't want him to waste the time. She didn't want to risk the extra time to give either one of them the opportunity to change their minds.

For encouragement, she rocked her hips. He thrust forward enough so the tip entered her. They both groaned. If it felt this good already, she was going to lose her ever-loving mind. They both moved again, pushing toward each other. Part of her wished he just drove inside, the other part savored his slow entrance.

"Grace," he breathed. His forehead dropped to hers. He braced his hands, one on the back of the ride, one on the safety bar. His chest heaved like it took great effort not to lose himself.

Tilting her hips more, she grasped his face and pulled his mouth down to hers. Before they touched, she murmured, "Rourke, please don't stop."

He withdrew, a wonderfully carnal sensation, but the feeling of loss was almost too much to bear. Stroking her with his tongue, he propelled forward, sliding in just an inch farther than he had been. They repeated the process until he was fully seated inside. She shifted her pelvis and rocked herself against him until she accommodated his girth.

It was more than she'd envisioned with Rourke. Cuddling, spooning, even hugging were things they'd have to work toward.

He withdrew from their kiss to nibble down her neck. "Are you ready, Grace?"

"*So* ready." She wrapped her legs around him, and the seams of his pants dug into her.

He drew back and thrust.

"Oh my—Rourke!" So. Good.

He rolled her shirt up until her breasts were bared and tugged her bra down. Her pebbled nipples aimed for the sky. He snagged a peak in his mouth. Only then did she let go of his shoulders and bury her hands in his hair.

In and out. Their ride seat swayed with the movement. He teased her breasts as his cock set fire to her. A slow bloom of heat spread from her center, flushing her body. When the orgasm hit, it was going to encompass her entire being.

In and out. The first ripples of climax gripped his shaft tighter. He released her nipple and reared back to watch himself impale her sex.

The look of awe across his face undid her. The reverence in his eyes, the rigidity in his torso, like he was stringing himself out to make this experience as long as possible.

Her inner walls clamped down on him. She couldn't hold back her explosion. Caressing his face once before she twisted her hands in his shirt, she threw back her head to cry out.

"Your ecstasy is breathtaking."

She only heard him. Her eyes were squeezed shut from the power, but his tone was full of disbelief.

He wrapped his arms around her legs to hold her still while he slammed into her one final time. He gritted his teeth and grunted his release. Rourke's shaft pulsing within her, his release spilling inside… She opened her eyes to watch while he was lost in orgasm. The characteristic calm of Ozias Rourke was gone, if only for a few seconds.

He sagged, breathing heavy. His hands were still clenched on the seat back and safety bar. Slight dents marred the metal under his fingers.

She relaxed back and loosened her hold on his shirt to stroke his face.

He flinched like he'd been burned.

Rapid footsteps approached their cove. The security guard.

His mask snapped back into place and he withdrew. Not bothering to shove himself back into his pants, he reached down to snatch her pants and shoes. Grace rearranged her bra and shirt until they were back in place.

The glare of a flashlight bounced off various surfaces of the ride.

Rourke dumped her clothing into her arms, then threaded his arm behind her and flashed them away.

Chapter Ten

Rourke released Grace after ensuring she was solidly on her feet.

"That was close," she muttered.

He'd flashed them to the area along the trail she'd fled to the first night. Early rays of dawn brightened the sky and he needed to get her to shelter.

When she shook out her pants to step into them, he finally adjusted his own clothing, which included restraining his nearly full again erection back behind the zipper.

He was still shaking.

Hellfire.

The embrace of Grace's body was unlike any he'd experienced. She was warm, receptive, and it'd been a long time since he'd been with a female who didn't crave pain with her pleasure.

Now he knew why. It was harder to maintain his distance when an inviting body beckoned him, offered comfort. He didn't want to get close to anyone. Didn't want the pretense of a relationship.

Not again. Not even if it was natural and not forced upon him.

Her beauty when she'd climaxed… The ethereal vision would haunt him for years. Soft, brown skin aglow in the moonlight. Her halo of hair and ridiculous zebra headband framed her face. And her curves…glorious. Most female vampires resembled runway models—long, lean, and defined. Grace outdid them all. He'd kill to see her lovely body, covered by nothing, strutting down his hallway every day of his long life.

Foolish fantasies for a foolish street rat. Bartering with the kid opened the floodgate to early memories. And that was *before* he'd been sold.

The idea of her as a true mate was pleasing enough, but his bonding instinct remained dormant. She admitted to being interested in him, but she would forever remain out of his league. A good-hearted, gracious female did not need to be attached to him, even if it was to while away the time until they met their true mates.

Grace moving on with a true mate? The low rumble of a growl escaped.

She glanced up from tying her shoe.

"We must return you to headquarters." *He* must return. His dirty secret of not being from a prime family revealed itself in his low tolerance of early daylight hours. Strong blood ran in his veins because he was a stubborn bastard. But without the extra power of prime, his time exposed to the weak rays of the sun was much more limited. Grace was younger and a commoner. She must already be uncomfortable.

Not that she seemed so. The shadows of the trees caressed her soft skin, still flushed with desire from what they'd done earlier. She straightened and he experienced a weird sensation, like his heart flipped. He rubbed his chest and grimaced.

"Are you okay?" Her golden eyes searched his with concern.

He was accustomed to his team checking on his well-being after a mission gone wrong, but to have Grace's regard…. *He* looked after her; it shouldn't be the other way around.

"Are you ready to flash back?"

She reluctantly nodded and threaded her arm through his.

After they entered headquarters, there was an awkward moment when they needed to go separate ways.

"I'll walk you to your room," he offered.

Her hand remained tucked around his bicep and he didn't encourage her to remove it.

She inhaled sharply and stopped. "You didn't tell me how Bishop was."

"Three against one is nothing for him."

Relief chased away the alarm in her expression, and they resumed along their path. Until she stopped again.

"And the boy? Has anyone found him?" Guilt crept into her eyes, like she was ashamed they'd been intimate at the fair while the young boy was still in danger.

"Bishop and Zoey are searching for him." Rourke didn't mention how he'd supplied them with plenty of information on slavers, and with immense gratitude, they didn't ask. "Demetrius is working the prime vampires we know are possessed."

Her eyes widened. "How many?"

What was better, tell her about blood slaves or discussing demon baits? "Six that we know of, but we're sure there's more." He continued toward her room, pulling her along. Her arm stayed in his and they both seemed to prefer it that way.

"How would they use the boy?"

"This boy is a commoner, but they may try what they'd do if they had a prime child. We've learned they can bind a child to a demon and when the child comes of age, he or she can be used to aid in the demon crossing to our realm. While the child is too young to repeat the bonding phrases, they can raise and groom him to gladly give himself up."

Grace's lovely body shuddered. "That's awful. If I can do anything to help find him, I will."

Her compassion floored him. He and his team dedicated their lives to help their people. It often served to provide him with several examples of the worst of the worst in all species. Vampires who sold their children, killed for power, killed for revenge, killed just because... Grace came from a good home. A commoner who'd lived a treasured normal life, but wasn't begging to return to one, everyone else be damned. She'd been dumped into this world, yet the boy topped her priority list.

Of course her situation and the child's were nearly identical.

They reached her door.

"Are you coming in?"

He should say no. Go back to his room. Recover from a mind-blowing quickie so he didn't sink further into Grace's orbit.

"Rourke," her voice dropped low, almost shy, "we didn't have a chance to do anything to mellow out after... Come in. I'll find something to eat and we can talk."

He didn't talk to his partners. He unlocked or unhooked them, zipped himself up, and left. But Grace wasn't a partner.

She was—what?

She dropped her hand from him and stepped inside. The ball was in his court.

He took a measured step inside, and she swung the door shut behind him.

The room had a more lived in feel than his did. Betty's handiwork was everywhere and Grace's presence capped it off.

She sorted through cupboards and drawers in the kitchenette. Cheese, crackers, and summer sausage were gathered into a pile on the counter.

"Have a seat." She slanted her head toward the small table.

She was feeding him. Again.

He frowned. He ate with people. Occasionally, he dined with them, but avoided that whenever possible.

Grace was serving him. Again.

"Did you cook and clean growing up?" He spoke to her delectable backside sticking out of the fridge door.

"Of course."

"It was expected of you?"

"As chores, yes. But also to teach us to be responsible adults."

She emerged with two beers and a pie.

Rourke freaking loved Betty's pies. It didn't matter what flavor. It didn't even matter what was inside because its only use was to hold the crust up.

His worthless mother never baked. His even more useless father never stepped foot into the kitchen. His masters only threw food at him.

She settled next to him and doled food out while peeking at him out of the corner of her eye. "This makes you uncomfortable."

He was embarrassed it was noticeable. "Yes."

She paused and faced him. "Did you have to…"

Before he could stop himself, the words spilled out. "I was a slave. In every sense of the word. One way to control me was through food. Otherwise, if my master wanted me to clean, I cleaned. If he wanted me to entertain, I danced. If he wanted blood, I offered my vein. If he wanted—" Rourke clamped his mouth shut.

Holy shit, he'd *never* admitted that to anyone.

Her hand rested on his. "It's okay, Rourke. I'd guessed as much from your peculiarities." A swell of the I-gotta-get-outta-heres welled up, but she distracted him yet again. "I want to go straight to dessert, but I know my stomach will get upset if I don't have something with substance in it. Dig in."

As Grace attacked her cheese and crackers, he eyeballed the pie. Betty made everyone a pie on their birthdays. He'd never told her when his was, but somehow a motherfucking pie showed up on his doorstep each year on the correct day.

"If you want a piece, go for it," Grace said around a mouthful.

Was his pie fixation obvious?

One deeply guarded secret of his was his love for sweets. He never indulged. It was hard enough to be civil and not tear into regular food like a caged beast.

Betty's infamous pies were the exception. No one insults the old vampire by not eating her baking.

Grace polished off her last cracker and produced a knife to cut the pie. He must've still been covetously staring at the dessert because she set the knife down and handed him a fork.

"I think we can work this off later."

His brows popped up at her suggestion and blood raged back to his dick. She wanted to have sex with him again. Of course his partners were always amenable to laying with him again, but he assumed it was because of the way he used the tools. Like Manka said, he was a good fuck.

When she saw he wasn't going to be the first to dig in, she stuck her fork in the middle and pulled out a heaping bite.

Sexual appetite mixed with sweet cravings while he watched the—hellfire, apple pie was his favorite—disappear between her pink lips.

Huge restraint. It took an enormous amount of self-control to secure his own bite and not tear into the thing with bare hands.

They ate in tense silence. As long as Grace continued, so did he. Soon they were scraping the bottom of the empty dish.

"Oh my god, that was delicious. It was homemade, wasn't it?"

He nodded, fighting back wild emotions. His belly was full of dessert, Grace's scent teased him and it was laced with his. The most powerful aphrodisiac *ever*.

"Ozias?"

His real name was a splash of cold water on his libido.

"You don't like that, I'm sorry. I think it's a cool name."

"No, it's nothing." Rourke kept everyone guessing what prime family he belonged to, and Ozias had a dump truck of memories attached. "But I prefer Rourke."

Her voice dropped to a husky growl. "What if I only say it in bed?"

That was it. His carnal need to fuck this female until she smelled like him, tasted like, and thought of only him roared back.

Standing up, he drew her up with him.

He systematically stripped her of every article of clothing and plucked her hair band out. Her desire clouded around him, whipping him into a frenzy. He forced himself to take a slow step back to view her gorgeous body.

High, rounded breasts strained for him with each breath. Her torso curved into a spectacular ass and strong, shapely legs. Curls framed her face, the color of a late summer sunrise: golden rays fading into the darker sky.

"You are amazing, angel."

Aw hell. She blushed.

"You don't believe me?" He closed the distance between them to gaze down on her.

"I feel like I'm seeing myself through your eyes when you look at me like that. I just never expected it from…"

He knew what she was getting at and he prepared to erect his walls. "A cold, unfeeling bastard."

"No." Her hand stroked down his cheek in a move she seemed to enjoyed doing. "Such a ferocious warrior. I'm so normal, and you're so… Look at the life you lead. I've seen those vampires in the club. Those females are your caliber. Not me."

"They have *nothing* on you, Grace. I could walk away from each one of them. And I did, many times. Our coupling was like a contract. I need this; you need that." His hands cupped her breasts, his thumbs circling her nipples. "I couldn't walk away right now if you shoved me out of the door."

She looked incredibly pleased, and that satisfied him. He wanted to please her, show her he wasn't trash.

"Can I take your shirt off?"

He tensed. He didn't do naked during sex—too much exposure. Opened the door and let the vulnerability right it.

"Just your shirt," she repeated. "You have an amazing body. I'd like to touch it while I'm riding you."

His shirt hit the floor. She chuckled. "Sit." He stiffened. "Please, and only if you want to."

Her hands hovered above his pecs, like she was waiting to see how he'd react.

The damaged vampire who had clawed his way to freedom rebelled at her requests and the loss of control.

But she said only if he wanted to. If he sat, her breasts would be closer to his mouth. He wanted.

His ass hit the chair.

"Do you want me to undo your pants or will you?"

He could kiss Grace's intelligence right now. She left everything up to him, but he'd acquiesce to whatever she wanted.

He flipped his button free and unzipped his leathers. His shaft throbbed against the material, but he left it in place.

"Sit on me, Grace." He tugged on her hand, not waiting.

She straddled him. He drew her head down for a kiss, and she exhaled into his embrace. Her hands roamed his chest and shoulders while his hands did the same to her. The touch of skin was as addicting as their pie. She was soft everywhere. He trailed his fingers farther down until he cupped her sex.

Her hips rocked to ride his hand. He swirled his tongue into her mouth and tunneled a finger between her folds. She was so wet. All for him. Her climaxes were a glorious thing to behold. He wanted to bury himself inside, but a front row seat to her release wouldn't be passed up.

A moan rewarded him when he found her clit. A few swirls and he stroked back until he entered her. The delightful squirm she did on his lap encouraged more. Soon, she set a pace, seeking the end she knew he'd give her.

But he held off. She broke their kiss to scowl at him.

"I want to watch you come, Grace."

"Then you need to let me."

The side of his mouth tipped up. "This is a pretty good show." *I don't want it to end.*

His almost smile sent a flood of juices to her center.

"My sexual frustration is what finally makes you smile," she said between gasps of pleasure.

"I didn't smile." But if this was her reaction, he might more often.

Her butt ground into his thighs as she desperately sought her orgasm. "Compared to your normal, that was a full out grin."

A laugh barked from a bona fide, albeit small, smile.

"Rourke—yes." She was coming. He redoubled his efforts, spearing her with a finger while his thumb excited her clit.

She leaned back to rest her hands on his knees as she rode through her peak. Breasts in his face, her melting in his hand, his desire to pleasure her *for* her, not because it was part of the arrangement, it was the most satisfying sexual experience he'd ever had. And the one earlier this evening provided a ton of competition.

The orgasm faded. He curled his other arm around her and she went lax. Removing his hand from her center, he pushed his pants down to release his shaft.

Just like that, she perked up.

Using him for purchase, she rose up and placed herself over the head of his cock. He used her new position to draw a taut nipple into his mouth. Her arms cradled his head and she slowly, savoring the feel, lowered herself onto him.

Just like before, her encompassing his length matched no other sensation he'd ever known.

Sex went beyond a basic need, a drive he couldn't ignore, to a recreational activity he could spend the rest of his life doing. As long as it was Grace he was thrusting into.

Completely within her, she swiveled her hips. His eyes damn near crossed.

His head cradled into her breasts, he was firmly within her embrace as she stroked herself up and down his length.

Such close proximity allowed him to feel her excitement, witness how her breaths caught and quickened when he thrust up into her. He'd never not cared about his partner's end of the encounter, but to be this close, to have so much influence on her body, it was empowering in a way his past had never allowed.

He encircled her waist with his hands and took over the pace. Grace was putty in his hands, trusting him to make her feel gooood—and he'd earn that trust.

She dropped her head down to whisper in his ear. "I can't believe how amazing it is with you. Everything just feels like more"

A new erogenous zone was created when she sucked in his earlobe and her teeth gently nibbled. He jerked and pumped her harder. Her breathy laugh tickled along the shell of his ear and his hands dug into her hips. He was going to explode and the force promised to blow his previous orgasm out of the water.

The naughty girl licked the rim of his ear. "I'm going to come."

Sharp moans turned into cries as she crested. He didn't want this moment to end, but his body had different ideas. His release shot through him until he clenched his jaw and threw his head back to roar her name.

They shook and shuddered into each other until his head sagged forward into her chest and she rested her cheek against the top of it. For a male who shunned intimacy, he suddenly needed her pressed against him, skin-to-skin.

A few seconds later, her head lifted. "I'm sorry, is this too much?"

He answered truthfully. "Not with you."

A smile touched her eyes and she finger combed his hair back. He closed his eyes and leaned into her touch.

"Want to take this to the bed?" she asked.

Did he? Yes, but…it wasn't *his* bed. Correlating with his physically suspended partners was his preference for his own bed. Strong preference.

Her shoulders drooped. He cursed himself for causing her reaction, it spurred him to stand. She squealed and clung to him.

"So that's a yes?"

"That's correct." He carried her back to her bed. After all, it's not like he would sleep.

***

Fyra gazed impassively at the pompous ass on the dais, whose fangs dripped yellow funk. Rancor sought to intimidate her.

It was working.

When the Circle wasn't happy, no demon was happy. Her eyes flittered over the piles of bones surrounding the throne he sat on. Hunks of meat hung off the fresh pile at his feet, aerating the room with eau de putrid funk. He used a phalange as a toothpick.

"Just so happens, Rancor, I was on my way to the earthly realm to harvest info from the vampire Bishop."

"Were you now?" his raspy voice drawled. His leering gaze slithered down her neck, skittered over her torso, lingering on an area she wished was invisible.

Her long fiery hair cascaded over her shoulders to cover her bare breasts, protecting them from his attention. She wasn't one of the ruling class of demons. She had a glorious humanoid body, if she did say so herself.

And she did. Often.

But times like this, it was more of a detriment than an aid. The ruling class, the Circle of Thirteen, took who they wanted, like, *what rape?* Usually, Fyra's feminine form was a turn off to the leathery bastards, but punishing her would be a great turn on and not on her end.

Why did angels get robes while demons only got loincloths? Like she'd hide that many weapons.

At her side stood Stryke, a fellow second tier demon with the same humanoid form, only male and hot as the devil. But he wasn't interested. She'd tried. At least before her current assignment.

Bishop Laurent.

Yummy. He ignored her summons, he hated her for binding him, and he was the best fuck she'd ever had.

When the Circle had first whored her out, or "utilized all her resources or she faced death" as they called it, she didn't want the assignment. She'd plotted ways for this Bishop to have an accidental beheading, just out of spite.

I don't fuck who I don't want to.

She had many more uses. Like brains. And, duh, she was named Fyra for a reason. Not only did she embody her name with her flaming hair and burning yellow eyes, but she was a steamy, crafty bitch.

Then she spied the big oaf and suddenly…*mission accepted.*

He despised her. She shivered with delight. Such a delicious emotion, catnip for demons.

Stryke threw her a look out of the corner of his eye that said *better you than me.*

Talk about crafty. He'd throw her under the bus in a heartbeat. See what she meant? The guy was sexy.

Back to placating Rancor. "I'm popping into Freemont hunting his big ass down. *Since I bonded him*." She laid that one on heavy because the Circle had an aversion to bonding. "I'll be able to find him wherever he is. He's had enough time to gather intel for me." If the second tier demons didn't do the dirty work for the Circle, they'd have been slaughtered for sport centuries ago.

Rancor eyed her suspiciously. Demons had award-winning resting bitch faces. "He defies you."

"He is powerful," she conceded, "but he was the easiest to entrap. Demetrius, well, we all know about him."

Rancor's six-inch-long fangs bared in a hateful grimace. Yeah, she'd totally rubbed that failure in.

To get back into his hateful graces, she justified her decision. "I wouldn't be able to get close to the one called Rourke in a human host. The little one, Ophelia, doesn't go for chicks. The other two, Zohana and Creed, who from their scents, are banging each other."

Stryke winced next to her. What was his problem? He might be a prude, the demon equivalent of a unicorn, but vampires liked to get busy and often. Which made Bishop such an essential target.

"Very well, then," Rancor snapped. "Come back with answers, or you'll hate life."

Ugh. She'd seen the Circle teach demons to hate life. Maybe she should take the focus off her, eh? The Circle was very peculiar about who was granted access to their exclusive cult on earth. Her class of demon couldn't possess just anyone to do their bidding.

Stryke was here because they had an assignment for him. But they didn't know about his unsanctioned activities topside. "I sure will return with answers. Hey, Stryke, will I see you wandering around up there again?"

"You bitch," he hissed for her ears only.

Laughing, she flipped him off and sauntered out. Their cult leader was supposed to have another voluptuous body lined up for her. Oh yes, she'd get answers out of Bishop.

Chapter Eleven

Grace woke alone in bed. Again.
Two days of passionate, ferocious love-making, and in the morning on both days, she'd awake to his absence.

It was more confusing than insulting. He'd opened up to her. Physically at least. She filled in the blanks where she could and gave him space. He'd been horribly abused. His rigidity around food and the fact he'd been at another's mercy went together. It was highly likely he either never got food or had to fight for it. Either way, he struggled to remain civilized. Eating Betty's pie with him, Grace had kept waiting for him to toss the dish across the room or fight for her fork.

Feeding from him again could wait. He hadn't offered; she hadn't insisted. Baby steps.

His cold demeanor hid a warm, thoughtful heart. After he'd come in from work the previous night, he'd taken her to her mom, dad, and Nathaniel's grave.

Surprising her with a visit to an unmarked gravesite.

Grace brushed a tear away. It was the most romantic thing he could've done. The next thing he could do would be to sleep in her bed. Or she in his, but she wouldn't force the issue. It'd come in time.

Just like this night she'd been dreading.

She had an appointment with Osiris tonight. If she didn't meet him, her parents who might not really be her parents could suffer.

Kicking her arm behind her head, she stared at the ceiling. Rourke's brother had given her two days to learn what she could in order to turn Rourke over.

It'd also given her time to think about his tame request. Why not just try to lure Rourke out for Osiris tonight?

No, the male had something else up his expensive sleeve.

She'd meet Osiris and tell him Rourke's habits—after omitting all the sex. Then she didn't know what she'd do. Or what would happen. Osiris may suspect she knew he was behind the attacks. Dare she leverage any info she had for Ari's whereabouts? Or would it only anger Osiris that he hadn't fooled her? Besides, what leverage? It's not like Rourke lived some secret agent lifestyle. He went to work investigating leads into the deaths earlier in the week. After her and Bishop's experience, she had stayed back at headquarters.

She and Calli researched a demon tome and journals that creeped Grace the hell out. A necessary experience because only she could remember what had happened in her life. Then she learned about the eyes going black when a demon possessed a vampire and put two-and-two together. Osiris was a host. Is that how he got the big house and expensive furnishings? Here's my body, now hand over the cash.

If Rourke was sold off, it fit that Osiris sold himself for buck or two, along with an unknown amount of power. Unless his parents sold him, too, but Grace got the impression he was older. Not exactly solid family morals roaming freely in that household.

She glanced at the time. One hour before she had to meet Osiris at the fair. He wanted her to wait by the Zipper where the stench of the rides and party goers would override his scent. It had worked before, but then she'd been covered in another guy's blood.

Her insides warmed when her mind surfaced the memory of her experience at the carnival with Rourke.

On a ride!

She'd better shower, or Osiris would smell Rourke all over her.

While under the spray and soaping her body, she plotted how she'd flash to the meeting spot. All she needed was an excuse to step outside. The rest she could explain easily enough. She'd been cooped up for days.

A big fluffy towel waited for her outside the door of the shower. She wanted to know where

Betty bought them and what she laundered them in. Grace was determined to find out. They were divine. The elderly vampire didn't need to clean up after her.

The cooking though. Betty could cook her old heart out.

Grace dried her face off and lowered to attend to the rest of her body when she caught Rourke resting against the door frame.

"Hey." Her heart rate sped up, but she was determined to remain calm. If they got busy, she'd still have time to pop out, but it'd be harder to step away from Rourke to leave for an hour without an ironclad excuse. She hated thinking in terms of deceiving him.

There was a slight crinkle at the corner of his eyes, an indication he was pleased to see her. His gaze roamed her curves. When a potent male like Rourke studied her body with heat in his eyes, she was loath to secure the towel around herself. Since he hadn't shown up again the last two evenings after he left her bed he must have a reason tonight.

"I have to go investigate another murder."

"Demons?" Her heart sank as guilt flooded her.

Osiris didn't orchestrate another killing so she'd have cover to get away, did he?

Why not? He'd allegedly killed at least three families that she knew of. It didn't wipe away the pit of responsibility that had settled into her gut.

"Yes. This time it's a member of a prime family. I think it's different from the others."

A wash of relief almost spiked her guilt. Like the death was of no consequence because it didn't involve her? She wasn't that person. "Prime family? Were the demons after a host?"

His expression was grim. "Likely. Would you like to come along?"

She blinked. Because her answer was yes. When had she become Grace Otto: CSI-Vampire? "No. I'd like to help, but I should catch up on lesson plans."

She'd already come to the forgone conclusion she had to drop tutoring. Her schedule these days didn't accommodate pre-arranged appointments.

He shoved his hands into his pockets and considered her. "You miss your work?"

Tapping a comb through her hair before she secured it back off her face, she formed her answer.

"Yes." The kids needed her. Sure they could get another tutor, but she abhorred abandoning them. "I miss the face-to-face time, but since I'm surrounded by people now, there's not a void to fill. I do enjoy teaching. Lesson plans aren't the same, but I still get to design them."

He contemplated so long, she wondered if she'd said something insulting. She was learning his peculiar mannerisms, reading the subtle nuances of his expressions, but much of him remained an enigma.

"We don't have people like you," he finally said. "Teachers. There's an academy the prime families attend. The rest of us are…homeschooled for lack of a better term."

If at all, hung off the end of his statement. Vampires couldn't attend elementary school, and unlike college courses, those classes weren't online or in the evening.

"Were you?" she asked quietly.

His expression darkened. "I was taught enough before… I've caught up since then."

Her admiration for him grew. "Maybe I need to start something." Her mind whirred, plans clicking into place, a list of supplies she'd need, the ages she could provide service for.

"You'd do that?" Genuine surprise emanated from him. "But you're here among the prime. You could even work for the academy."

"Sounds like they have what they need if they're in an established school catering to the prime families." It'd even be up her alley. Her tutoring catered to children who struggled with the basics, anywhere from science to math to reading. Whatever the parents hired her for.

"They always have what they need."

Telling words. Both his tone and use of "they." He'd been part of "them" for forty years, but still didn't consider himself part of the crowd.

"I'm a commoner, too."

A glint of humor entered his eyes. He stepped forward to kiss her on the forehead, the sweetest gesture he'd given her yet. "You're anything but common, Grace."

When he left, his absence carried all the warmth from her shower with him. Cool air snaked over her bare shoulders. She suppressed a tremor at the foreboding sense carried on the draft. Now, to figure out how to sneak around behind his impressive back.

***

Bishop stiffened as another siren song filled his head.

That damn demon summoned him relentlessly. And it didn't help her husky voice inspired wet dreams.

The piece of shit he was talking to glanced around, noting his reaction.

"Go on," Bishop prompted as if nothing was wrong.

Going on two nights and they hadn't found the kid. Much like human time frames for missing children, each day that passed spelled a worse outcome for the child.

The thug Bishop had hunted down earlier was lying through his teeth, but Bishop sensed he didn't know anything. The male was mostly concerned with protecting himself and his own in underhanded dealings.

Bishop held up a hand to stop him. "Pilsner, do you or do you not know of any vampires looking to market children?"

"No, Master Laurent, no one's approached me for documents for a minor. I swear to you, I wouldn't provide service to any who'd mean our young harm."

Unless the price was right. They often hit Pilsner up for information, and with a certain level of bribery, he was very accommodating—to an extent. Pilsner protected his revenue stream. He'd never turn in his client base. But he'd gladly turn over those who interfered with business, and customers who brought Demetrius and his crew knocking on his door fit the bill.

"You know how to reach me if you hear anything."

Bishop ignored the sniveling male and stalked away. His demon-bitch-induced migraine blocked out the words.

Before he met up with Rourke at the latest crime scene, Bishop roamed the quiet streets. He didn't get out much lately. It shamed him he was relieved Grace's drama redirected his team's focus from his unusual behavior. Hanging out in his place watching movies shouldn't be a cause for concern, but he'd been known for how frequently he fed his baser drives.

At least until that demoness tricked him. He shook his head, his body growing to half-mast hearing her sultry voice float through his mind. Since he couldn't cruise the social scene for sex, he was reduced to jerking off to her summons. Adding salt to a wound didn't begin to describe it.

Rubbing his forehead, he glanced up before he wandered into trouble with either humans or vampires.

An attractive woman sauntered toward him. Any other night, pre-bonding, she would've turned his head. Not the normal sexpot who approached him at the clubs, she possessed the curves and the stature he looked for.

I choose what you like, Bishop.

Oh, fuck.

He slowed to a standstill. She approached, her eyes reflecting her delight.

"It's you, isn't it?" His body knew the answer. Their bond electrified his nerves, until he was aroused to painful levels.

"Bishop." The human's voice purred. Pleasant enough, but not sex to his ears like the one in his head. "I'm flattered you recognized me."

She curved an arm into his. He jerked as if shocked. Their connection had grown even stronger. He followed as she led him into the darkened entry of a store. To any onlookers, they'd appear to be any other couple trying to sneak a quiet moment.

He pried her off and pushed her to one side as he stepped back to the other. "What do you want?"

Those pretty red lips pouted. She eyed him coyly and fingered the low slung collar of her wrap dress. "I take care of you. You must be starving."

He was. Hunger roared so sudden he slammed himself against the wall of the cove to keep from jumping the woman. As much as he wanted to throttle the demon until she turned blue and her head popped off, he wouldn't hurt an innocent human, not even one who was dumb enough to play with demons.

She swiveled her hips. "What's wrong, my big strong male? This host knew what to expect when I took over…mostly."

"You lie to them." He didn't have to ask. Demon equaled lie.

Her cunningness shone through the host's brown eyes. "You think so little of me. She was told I needed her to talk with a vampire."

"You'd use her body to fuck me."

The demon dramatically rolled her eyes. "Please. The idea of feeding a vampire thrills her. Why do you think these little pretenders flock to— well it doesn't matter."

Note to self: find the fucker who recruits the hosts and rip his fucking head off. "Feeding, demon. Not fucking."

The pout returned. "She'll feel nothing but pleasure, and you excel at that Bishop."

His body screamed *yes I do, yes I do*. Her proximity was making him go haywire.

She waved her hand to change the subject and adopted an enticing simper. "Anyway, I'll feed you after you tell me all the juicy news happening in your world."

"I will tell you nothing."

"Aww, Bishop. That's cute, but I need to hear all the details." She thrust her breasts out, as if that was all it took for him to turn on his team.

He said nothing.

The teasing grin fell from her face. "I need you to talk. All of it."

Driven to obey her command, his mouth opened. He snapped it shut.

"Come on, come on, Bishop. What do you and your fearless leader Demetrius know about demons, huh? What is he planning?"

All the information poured into his head, pushing to get out. He had an urgent need to tell her about the tome Calli found in her dad's possession, the murders they were investigating, the families they knew who hosted one of the thirteen.

He gritted his teeth. No! His friends were his family. His job encompassed the entirety of his being. None of them would be lost this way.

"Bishop," her voice had an edge, "tell me everything."

The words danced on his tongue, coaxing it to wind itself around each syllable and pass them onto her.

"Tell me, vampire."

Strangling sounds crawled out of his throat. He choked them back down.

"No."

Her eyes grew wide in disbelief, then narrowed in determination. "Tell me, Bishop."

He fought back the urge. "No." She opened her mouth to command him again, but he laid a finger over her lips. Desire flared deep in her gaze. "I don't turn on my friends. Gut me, torture me, send me to Hell, *I won't say a word*."

His finger dropped, and he waited for her tirade, her commands.

She blinked. Blinked again. "Do you think for one minute any of them would remain loyal to you?"

It wasn't a sneer or a statement of derision. She was genuinely curious.

"Absolutely."

The demon drew back like the concept was foreign to her. Her world must be a very miserable place. A tendril of compassion snaked through his heart, and he stomped that shit back in place.

She was a demon whose goal was to destroy his team, his friends, him.

"What's your name?" he asked.

A conniving smile twisted her lips. And she was back. "You want to learn about me, vampire? After your disobedience, I will reward you with nothing."

"I'll find someone else to feed on."

A flare of jealousy passed through her expression. Her smile faltered.

Interesting. He'd use it. "I'll find someone else to fuck while I'm at it."

A flush pressed up through the human's cheeks, beads of sweat broke on her forehead. A wave of heat pressed toward him. The girl looked like she had a sunburn. The demon's power was behind it and if she didn't cool off, she'd kill the human host.

His softer side won out over cruelty. "Fine. I'll feed from you…if you tell me your name."

The heat dissipated. Her threat of not giving him a vein turned empty once he'd threatened to go elsewhere to feed. His gut twisted. Even the human's body didn't appeal to him like it should.

She wiped her sweaty forehead off and studied him. "No name. You've been a bad boy."

He growled with frustration. Why was her name so critical anyway? Demon fit her just fine. "Why hide it, demon? We knew Draken's name when he went after Calli."

Her features clouded over at Draken's name. Bishop catalogued that for later. Everything learned about his demon would help his plight.

Her fingers twiddled and she shifted her stance. The first signs of true emotion she'd ever expressed. Or she could be fucking with him.

"Draken was a little too single-minded." A grin transformed her back to the trickster she preferred. "I have plans for you. Come." She waved him toward her and bared her neck. "Feed."

His fangs throbbed. His hunger suddenly didn't care he wasn't crazy about feeding off the human. "We are bound. Why don't you cross in your true form, why use hosts?"

Her throaty laugh went straight to his cock. "The human world can't handle me."

Irritated at his body's reaction around her, he struck. She purred her approval and hugged his head to her neck.

Damn, he should've used her wrist. The lush body rubbing against him threatened to override his good sense. No! He wouldn't take the human. Blood he needed to fight the demon, and it might as well be from a human who allegedly catered to cult life.

His demon reached for his fly, but he shifted. She tried again. Bishop swallowed one more mouthful and closed the wounds. He batted her hands away from his crotch. An idea formed in his mind. His demon had a thing for him. She targeted him, stalked him, and the sex she wanted from him with each encounter was about her, not about using and abusing the hosts' bodies.

He pinned her against her side of the cove, towering over her. Confidence slipped from her expression and her pupils dilated. Oh yes, she wanted him.

"The next time we fuck, demon, it'll be with your real body." His shaft screamed its approval at the thought. Fucking bond. His demon shouldn't be able to string his libido along like a marionette.

"Be careful with the game you play." She cupped his manhood, her approval written in her sultry smile. "You want to fuck the real me?"

"No," he snarled.

The tendril of a lie wafted up to his nose. Hellfire! She controlled him so completely he was turning on himself.

She threaded her hands around his neck. He resisted her attempt to draw his head down to her lips. "I'll let you have the real me. Just tell me what you know about my world."

The words welled up. He quashed them back down. "No."

Heat assaulted him. She was irate.

No, not just angry. The look in her eye was also…worried?

"I'll sever our bond," she offered. "Give me something to take back."

To be free of her? He should rejoice. Instead his libido mourned the loss of connection before she'd even followed through.

But…he'd never turn on his people. The drawback of a human host was how it dulled the senses. At least, he assumed it would. And he wouldn't need to lie completely, just feed her impertinent information.

"You'll free me?"

Meeting his gaze, she said, "I swear."

Hope surged, but still…she was a demon.

He pretended to think about it when he was really trying to figure out what to tell her. "We're trying to learn about your world, but we don't have much to go on. Draken told us things when he was chasing Calli."

She made a disgusted sound. "He always liked displaying his power. What did he say?"

"He could bond and cross into our plane in his true form." He omitted the part where having a baby with his bonded would allow him a free pass to cross back and forth, even after the Circle had secured their thirteen hosts and ruled the earthly plane.

"What else?"

"He kept asking us where the book is." Total lie. "We've determined it's like an instruction manual on demons, and we'd like to possess it." Not an untruth. They certainly would like to keep it.

"Why would Draken have thought you had it?"

He shrugged like it wasn't a big deal. "I guess Calli's mother was big into your world, a power hungry bitch." His demon nodded like she approved of what Calli's mother had done. "We don't know what she did with it."

"How many hosts to the Circle do you know about?"

What should he tell her? "If they weren't involved in Calli's abduction to hand her over to Draken…" He shrugged, letting her think it so he didn't risk a lie. "Now free me."

"Oh my dear Bishop. You're mine."

She waved a hand in front of his face, and like before, he slipped into unconsciousness and crashed to the pavement.

Chapter Twelve

The carnival was going full force when Grace flashed to the approved section Osiris had shown her. No brimstone-laced scent lingered. She must've arrived first.

Her sneakers whispered across the pavement as she entered the throng of fair-goers. The few dollars she'd thrown into her pocket burned a hole with each game she passed. Especially the darts. All night wouldn't be enough to stand there and pop balloon after balloon until she upgraded to the four-foot plush unicorn, and repeat.

She wove her way through giggling couples. A ping of longing hit her. She touched the spot on her forehead where Rourke's lips might as well have branded her. Screams swirled from the ride she approached. Metal cars swung around an elliptical path, rocking and swinging on a rotating oval boom.

There he stood, gathering his share of admiring glances from the single ladies in the crowd.

How he and Rourke resembled each other. Same tall, fit body, same broad shoulders tapering to a lean waist. The dark hair and nearly black eyes cinched the similarities, but Grace knew better. Rourke's dark coffee irises still weren't demon black like she'd seen his brother's turn.

Then there was the smile. As much as Grace would love to put one on Rourke's face, she'd do without until it was real. Osiris's was not.

Dressing down today, Osiris? If he was attempting to blend in, his burgundy silk button up and pressed slacks were a fail. They made an odd pairing with her worn and comfortable jeans and hoodie. The chill in the air required a sweater. Vampires still got cold. The demon within Osiris must offer him heat to wear a thin shirt like that.

"Grace."

His false smile set off an itch between her shoulder blades, like she was a target. Which she guessed she was.

"Osiris." She struggled to keep her tone neutral. He couldn't know she suspected him of all the murders, but she couldn't appear to betray Rourke so easily. Not after Osiris hinted at a deeper connection between her and Rourke.

So badly, she wanted to trade the location of her possible birth parents for the location of the missing child. With their picture in mind, she could've approached Rourke and Demetrius about finding them. But the request would reveal she didn't buy Osiris's bullshit, and by default, that she knew he was behind the murders.

"Walk with me, Grace. Tell me everything you've learned."

He flared an elbow out like she was supposed to hook on to it. She shoved her hands in her pockets instead.

His deep chuckle would be sexy, if he wasn't evil. "Don't tell me my brother's winning you over with his lies."

"I'm being cautious on both accounts."

"Even though he's taken everything away from you?" His tone was cool. "Twice?"

"That remains to be confirmed."

"He's responsible. Trust me."

She almost scoffed, but no wave of lies hit her nose. Her brows drew in. Confidence Rourke wasn't involved dropped to *pretty* sure he wasn't involved. Argh! She was a school teacher—intrigue was not her forte.

"I don't trust either of you."

His cocked eyebrow. No lie emanated from her and that cracked a fissure in her heart. This evening when she woke, albeit alone, she would've confirmed she undoubtedly trusted Rourke. Yet, Osiris's words ate away at her confidence—like he'd intended them to.

She just didn't know what Rourke's role was in everything. It's not because she thought he really stole her families from her.

As they strolled, she reported Rourke's routine the last two nights. Humans sauntered past, oblivious to the paranormal creatures among them. She was no threat to them, but Osiris, she imagined would kill them indiscriminately.

"Are you ready for your next assignment, my dear?"

"I'd like to meet my parents." Another itch settled in between her shoulder blades. She checked the crowd to see if someone was watching her.

"All in good time. My brother is still at large, putting any kin of yours in danger." His gaze also roamed the throng of people, like he sensed something was unsettling her.

If Osiris wasn't responsible for her tickling sensation...what was going on?

"Can I at least see them? In person, so I know they really are still alive?" *And I can lay my eyes on them and know I'm not alone.*

She interpreted his lack of a decline as a positive sign. "Fine. I'll take you to their home now. But you must promise me something in return."

Whatever he asked couldn't be good. She peered up at him from the corner of her eye. "What?"

"You must swear to repeat what I say."

"What?" Swearing anything around this male was a tricky prospect. Kind of like making a deal with the devil.

"I have a phrase you'll need to repeat for me, to swear I can trust you in this. Stopping Ozias's reign of destruction is of the utmost importance."

Like hell. Rourke was involved, but not in the killings. "How about I promise to think about it?"

A flurry of activity dragged Grace's attention to her left. A security guard was squinting at her under the bright fair light, and the man she had an unfortunate incident with a few nights ago was pointing at her.

"Oh shit." Resisting the temptation to flash immediately, she spun and walked swiftly through the throng of people.

"Hey!" the guard shouted.

"Grace." Osiris easily caught up with her and wrapped his hand around her bicep. "Friends of yours?"

"I, uh…he thinks I tried to mug him."

He threw his head back and laughed. "How interesting."

She was tempted to peek at him, just to see how Rourke would look freely displaying humor.

When his laughter died, she glanced at him and didn't care for the wicked gleam in his eye. Since he hauled her faster through the crowd, she had no choice but to go with him.

"Don't hurt them."

"Why on earth would you think that?" His innocent tone missed the mark.

"We're faster and stronger. We can get away." Defending herself was one thing, senseless violence against humans wasn't in her plans for the night.

"Ma'am." The guard's shadow fell across her. She sped up, indiscriminately pushing the young and old out of her way.

Osiris released her arm and confronted the guard. She only heard syllables muttered, but whatever he said stopped the guard's pursuit. What were the chances Osiris would only trance him and not cause bodily harm?

Picking her pace up to a trot, she wove through the carnival trailers, frantic to get to a concealed area she could flash from.

A dark form curved around one of the trailers. It was the human, her botched meal from the other night, and he was angry.

"I don't know what your boyfriend told the guard, but I won't let you go so easily."

Stupid, idiotic, moron. "You need to leave," she hissed. "I don't know what he'll do to you."

A moment of indecision passed through his features. Not even he could argue with the sincere desperation in her voice.

"Y-You beat the shit out of me." He backed up when Grace sensed Osiris approaching behind her, a masculine presence similar to Rourke. "I knew you'd come back to prey on another Joe. I came every night to stop you."

His misplaced valor might get him killed.

Osiris stalked past her, but she slapped her hand on his chest. A growl escaped, vibrating under her fingers.

"As you can see," she tried to catch the man's eye for any persuasion she could use, "I'm tricking no one tonight, but you might get hurt again. Leave, while only your pride is damaged." And seriously, she hadn't mugged him for real.

Osiris's hard chest quivered, like he'd been predicting serious violence and she'd thwarted his anticipation. His powerful muscles didn't turn her on in the slightest. If it had been Rourke's chest she was attached to, well, it'd be a different story.

The guy's eyes darted back and forth between her and Osiris. Anxiety wafted off of him in increasing quantities. Eventually, it won over male ego and he took off back around the trailers.

She dropped her hand from his chest. Osiris snatched it up and nipped at her finger.

A yelp escaped her. She tugged her hand back to her side.

His chuckle irritated her as much as it filled her with alarm.

"Grace. You're a puzzle. One moment, I could swear you're terrified of me, the next, you act like you could take my head and drop kick it across the room without raising your pulse."

But all the moments with him scared her. "I'd like to see my parents now."

"Alas, I cannot go with you in case Ozias smells me on you. Therefore, I'll take your oath before I give you the address."

"That's not how this was supposed to work."

"Grace." His tone and his nearly black eyes were full of warning.

"Look. I can't afford to be stupid. Yes, I'd love to find out my parents are alive. But it'd be terribly impulsive if I trusted you completely, just like it'd be rash if I accepted everything Rourke tells me."

"Rourke." He bit off the word with complete hate. "He goes by that name to fool people. Did you know that? I hear no one mention the commoner Rourke, who was accepted into the inner ring of Demetrius and his prime fold. Why? Because he won't own up to who he really is and lets everyone assume he has a fancy-dancy prime last name."

Rourke didn't spill his first name readily, so she shouldn't trust him about anything? Did Osiris think she was born yesterday?

Of course, if he was older than Rourke, she was much, much younger than him.

Osiris snatched her arms and dragged her close. Eyes wide, she swallowed hard when her gaze landed on black, soulless irises.

"I'm being more than patient with you, Grace." A wild beast had replaced Osiris. Even his voice had dropped to a guttural rumble. "If you want to see your parents alive, you need to swear to me you'll do as I say."

Fighting against panic, she steadied her words. "Isn't Rourke the danger to them."

The demon within Osiris lowered his head, his hot breath caressed her face. She wanted to vomit.

"I'm not as gullible as my host Osiris is. You've been playing him. I can smell his brother on you." He sniffed again like he was tasting her, and she *felt* it. She shuddered. "I can smell him in you. I would bet Osiris's left nut you're his brother's true mate."

She stiffened. True mate? But Rourke didn't feel it, or he didn't act like it. Her mind clicked through all the info she'd learned with Calli. Once true mates crossed paths, they couldn't get aroused by any others and feeding became an issue.

Maybe true on her end, but his?

The demon shook her, yanking her attention back to him. "I repeat, your parents' life for your words. It's simple."

"What will those words do?" Terror laced her whispered question.

"Let me know I can trust you." The black grew to encompass the whites of Osiris's eyes.

"H—How?"

He bared his fangs. "Say them, or they die."

Tears welled. She'd been too young to save the two she thought were her mom and dad, but they had died saving her. She'd been too late to do anything about her human parents and brother. This demon offered her another opportunity, but it came weighted with many unknowns—and none of them good.

The demon breathed into her ear. "I know you don't believe Osiris. I know you think he killed the humans. And you're right."

The tears spilled, streaking fire down her cheeks. Having it confirmed made it real. "Why?"

She jerked back when he licked a tear off her cheek. Her arms were still in his iron grip. She'd have bruises for hours before she healed.

"Because of you."

The struggle drained out her. "Osiris said Rourke was involved."

"For him, yes. For us, we wanted you." He grinned broadly. "And here you are. Unless you want more of your loved ones to die, including that little boy you think you can save?"

No, not him, too. Her eyes squeezed shut.

"Yes, Grace. Him, too. Repeat after me."

***

Rourke roamed through the lower level of the upscale estate, noting important details. Class oozed from the furnishings and the expensive decorations, even through the blood splattered across them.

Creed and Zoey had arrived with him, but they'd split to search all the levels. These kinds of dwellings, the ones of the rich and powerful vampires, were mansions with a large, stately outer appearance. The mansions were used to conduct business during the night and contained at least one ornate level below for daytime.

Two bodies were in the lower level. Vampires who'd been ripped apart and drained of blood like it'd been shaken out of them.

Creed approached from behind, his usual jovial expression grim. "The servants were wiped out. Two maids and a butler. I'd say they didn't know it was coming. The butler and one maid were still in bed. The second female was felled at the door of her bedroom. She must've heard something wrong and got up to investigate. The perpetrator took out the prime mom, dad, and daughter first." He pointed to the remnants as he mentioned them. "Then took the servants by surprise. They fought back the best they could, but it did no good."

"How'd the servants die?"

The male scratched the back of his neck and scanned the gruesome scene. "Ugly, but more merciful than the primes. He incapacitated them before he beheaded them."

Rourke nodded. The primes had suffered. The limbs were ripped off, and if Rourke read the damage to the arms correctly, he'd say the victims were beaten with them before being graciously beheaded.

Whoever carried out the killings either did it for sport and wanted the gruesome evidence discovered, or they were too chicken shit to pack stakes to dust them. The problem with vampires arming themselves with stakes is the risk of having them taken and used against them. Not much fighting happens after you're reduced to a pile of ash.

Zoey entered. She and Creed often partnered together, on and off duty. Rourke stayed out of it, but Demetrius grumbled about how it'd bite them in the ass. For the most part, none of them fraternized, but he couldn't blame Zoey. Losing her true mate the way she had, she turned to a male she felt safe with.

Like he had with Grace.

"I know these primes." Zoey's serious brown eyes absorbed the scene. "Went to school with their son…whose body is missing. Since he's not here and the rest of them are, down to every last drop, he's the prime suspect—no pun intended."

"And we can all smell what the root of the conflict was," Rourke said.

Their heads bobbed in agreement. Sulfur saturated every fiber in the room.

Creed crouched by a large scorched area in the main rug. "Accidental summons or intentional?"

Zoey made a disgusted noise. "Knowing Peter, their son I went to school with, it was intentional. He was always the entitled type."

Both Creed and Rourke raised an eyebrow at her.

"Well," she clarified, "more than the usual sense of entitlement we have."

We, of course, didn't include Rourke. All he was entitled to was revenge on his dear brother.

Rourke broke apart from them, crossing the room. "I went through their office, all their documents, but I think Peter's room needs a closer look."

All three of them descended on the son's room. Everything was overturned: the dressers, the closet, the mattresses. Creed jumped on top of the furniture to search the vents.

"Bingo." Creed extracted a thumb drive. "Digital evidence, my favorite."

"There's a laptop in the girl's bedroom." Rourke ran to grab it.

Creed's love for electronics grew with each decade until he was downright giddy with each new invention. Rourke had a smartphone that was smarter than him. It was all he'd tolerate. Creed lined up for each new version of anything starting with "i" or he paid a human to do it if it was during daylight hours.

His friend busted through the password requirement which would've made Rourke tap out immediately. Once the drive was plugged in, Creed sifted through documents. Zoey peered over Creed's shoulder with Rourke.

"Looks like someone had an interest in the occult," Zoey muttered.

Screenshots that'd been saved of various demon mythology comprised several files. Then an interesting website.

"We'll have to get this to Calli. She can determine which websites are correct and which are just human fantasies."

"Lookit." Creed sat back so they both could see. "I pulled up a website Peter had saved. I mean, I don't know if it's legit, but it seems real as hell. Pun totally intended."

Rourke scanned the page. "Is that an advertisement for a cult?"

"I know, right?" Creed barked a laugh and folded his hand behind his head. "I mean, it's like 'Cult Leaders 'R' Us: We got all sorts of demons, all the time.' What idiot is this bold?"

Zoey scrolled through the site. "Terrance Walkins has the balls we're looking for." She straightened. "It's getting too close to daylight. Rourke, tomorrow night, you and Bishop get out to go shake this guy down. Creed and I will take this back to Calli and arrange for the cleaning of this place to put it up for sale."

Rourke didn't envy the vampire crew that swept through places like these, cleansing them from floor to ceiling, and "rehousing" all the belongings. The items were sold and the crew they hired got to pocket the earnings, as long as it was cleared through Demetrius.

Bishop. His closest friend was acting weird again. Holed himself up in his room with an excuse along the lines of "blood meal not sitting well."

As Rourke wove his way out into the night, images of a naked Grace emerging from the shower earlier arose. He intensely anticipated his return home into her arms, the slow plunge of her fangs into his vein had teased him since the night he'd fed her.

Before daylight, he'd feel it again.

Chapter Thirteen

Rourke stood outside Grace's room and nearly choked. An herbal smell so strong he had to take a step back hung like a dark cloud in front of her door. Was she burning incense?

He knocked.

No answer.

Tilting his ear toward the door, he listened. It was quiet, but he sensed her inside.

He knocked again. "Grace?"

The movement from within sounded…watery? Then a shuffling of bare feet on carpet carried closer to the door.

The door opened to reveal Grace, once again clad in nothing but a towel, droplets of water sluicing down her torso.

The pungent fog of incense nailed him. He sneezed. She jumped and clutched her towel so tight her knuckles turned white.

"Oh, sorry. I extinguished it a while ago." She stayed in the opening, blocking his entrance. "Everything was catching up to me and I went to the fair again to relax. But I stunk when I left, I wanted to…smell like something else."

He surveyed her fist still on her towel, her brown eyes darting from the wall behind him to her feet then to his boots. "Is everything all right?"

Deep creases of weariness settled into her expression. "I hope it will be. I'm sorry, Rourke. I think I just need to crawl into bed today and sleep it off."

He dropped a kiss onto her forehead, stuffing down another sneeze. Had she bathed in pure lavender essential oil?

"Good night, Grace. Call if you need me." His head hung down in thought on his way back to his flat.

Severe disappointment. So that's what it felt like. He missed Grace, and he'd continue to miss her while he slept alone in his bed. Not just sex, but her laying in his arms, listening to her soft breaths while she slept spooned into him like before.

Once he'd even drifted off himself, only to jolt awake, almost rousing her. He'd shushed her back to sleep and beat feet back to his room and the safety of his mattress, where he couldn't drift off because she wasn't there.

It'd be the same tonight.

***

On heavy legs, Grace plodded back to her bedroom. Her shoulders hung as if the weight of the compound hung on them, which made sense.

After all, she was now a two for one deal.

Will not cry!

No demon was squeezing tears out of her. They shared the same body. The demon bitch—what had Osiris's own demon called her?—could take over at any time. Like she had when she first entered Grace.

God, she didn't remember any of it. Her only solace was if Rourke was her true mate and the reason for her recent feeding struggles, not even the demoness could choke down another's blood or be driven to violate Grace's body.

The first thing Grace recalled after she spoke the dreaded oath was hearing Rourke knock. She came awake and it all flooded back—Osiris's demon and her stupid optimism thinking she could help Ari and find a way out, before she lost all control of her own actions.

Fuck!

She dressed into her pajamas. Perhaps she could raid the tome and find a way to expunge this thing from her. Would she have time today before Calli returned to study it for the evening?

Grace slipped into the hallway. If she tiptoed, she'd look guilty as fuck. The more she considered finding the tome, the more it made complete and absolute sense, like it was the best idea in vampire history. Her muscles trembled as she reined her urge in to dart from corner to corner until she reached the large makeshift library that had been converted to Calli's office.

Of course it would be locked. Why hadn't she thought of that?

Rourke's handsome face materialized in her mind. He'd have lock picks, but this lock was electronic. Oddly, he hadn't engaged in hacking those types of locks. Too different from the ones that had held him captive, perhaps.

The door suddenly opened. Grace jumped back with a gasp.

Calli smiled in reassurance. "Sorry to startle you. What are you doing here so early?" She glanced at the clock. "Or late, depending on how you look at it."

"There's some demon…things…that have been bothering me." Truth. "I hoped to scour for answers, see if anything popped out now that I've had more time to absorb it all since we went over it." Mostly truth.

"Absolutely." Calli propped the door open with her hip. "Go through my notes and see what you find."

Grace nimbly moved past her, pressing against the door frame. A funny look flittered through the other female's features.

"Is that lavender bubble bath or perfume?" Calli stayed in the doorway.

Chitty chat-chat wasn't on Grace's radar, but she exuded politeness and refrained from slamming the door out of Calli's grip to shut herself in alone. "Essential oil bath salts. Would you like to try some sometime?"

Calli's aquamarine gaze remained congenial, though her stance was more serious. "Of course. I love lavender. Talk to you later, Grace."

"Thanks, Calli."

When the door finally clicked closed, Grace sagged with relief. These people were her friends, took her in when she'd lost everything. Now she was the most dangerous thing under the roof.

Her resolution to get the monstrosity out of her reaffirmed, she dove into Calli's journals. Paging through binders of Calli's printed notes, she searched for any indication there was an incantation to remove the demon.

No luck. She found the very words she'd spoken earlier, but nothing to undo them.

A frantic drive to find the tome rose with in her. She must find it. Must. Now.

Grace shook her head. Yes, she'd come down there for that, but Calli was thorough. If she'd found the anything worthwhile in the tome, it was in her notes.

Need the tome. NOW!

Instant headache.

Oh god. It was the demon screaming through.

Grace's eyesight began to dim, the edges becoming hazy like the enhancements in a photograph.

No, no, no. The battle for control of her body quickly swung in favor of the demon. A tear of desperation almost squeaked out before she lost entirely.

***

"Grace?" Rourke's voice cut through to Grace.

Abruptly awareness flooded back as the demon relinquished control of her body. Ripped sheets of paper surrounded her, covering the desk and the floor. Her chest heaved, like she'd been exerting herself enough to breath heavily.

How much time had passed? Holy shit, were those all of Calli's notes?

She spun slowly. Rourke stood in the room, Demetrius next to him, Calli was still in the hallway. Calli's mouth was pulled down in a frown, her expression full of guilt and concern.

"Grace, did you do this?" Rourke asked. His expression was carefully blank, back to the cold slate he'd been when they met.

Swallowing the giant lump in her throat, she again assessed the damage. The laptop lay against the wall where it had fallen after she apparently tossed it. Likely because the demon couldn't hack into it. Cabinet doors hung ajar, some ripped off entirely. Drawers were dumped, books shredded. Nowhere did she see the tome she and Calli had once bent over.

Calli interpreted the harried search. "The tome is under lock and key. Only available for those who need to know the location."

"Good." The word escaped Grace and gave her an idea. She spoke before the demon interfered. "I'm possess—" It was like a hand bitch-slapped her brain. "So's Osiris."

She gaged. Her throat closed up. She worked her lips to mouth the words, but she gaped for air instead. The demon was going to strangle her from the inside out. Dropping to her knees, she fought with all her might. One more sentence!

"Birth…" She coughed, blood-tinged sputum hit the floor. "Parents…alive—"

For the third time since she threw everything away with the best intentions, she was pushed back by the demon.

Chapter Fourteen

R ourke couldn't tear his stunned gaze off Grace. Her agony tore him up inside, but he couldn't get close. Not when he suspected what had happened.

Well, he more than suspected. She just told them. Possessed.

Her lovely face glared up at him, her eyes completely black.

"You have us at a bit of a disadvantage." Demetrius sounded casual, but his stance was anything but. "Your name is?"

Grace bared her fangs and snarled.

"I'm sorry, I didn't catch that." Demetrius maintained eye contact with the demon who'd hijacked Grace.

Desperation to save her should've taken priority, but he couldn't shake the fact she had to have uttered the bonding spell. Had it been willingly? The words don't accidentally spill out. Part of him screamed it didn't matter. It was Grace, and he had to save her. The other part filled with rage she might've and trotted danger into his home, among his family.

Then her last words sunk in. Birth parents alive. No matter how he felt, he needed answers. His emotions could eat shit until he knew what happened to Grace and why. The demon within her held the answers.

He glanced at Demetrius to make sure they were on the same page. They had worked together for a long time, their routine second nature. His friend was the distraction, Rourke inched to the side, the best they could do at surrounding the demon.

"Demetrius," Grace's lip curled in a sneer. "I will enjoy killing you. After I rend all the limbs from your love's…" The demon retched on the word. "…body."

"At least you'll smell good doing so." Demetrius's hands flared out in a defensive position, in case a weapon was needed, but like Rourke, he didn't want to hurt Grace in the scuffle. "The stench of your new bath products gave you away, made Calli suspicious. Other than you arriving at her office in the middle of the day to search our records when Grace is usually in Rourke's arms."

Damn right she had been. Rourke was pissed at himself for not catching on earlier when he'd spoken to her. He'd grown too close to Grace, her impromptu aromatherapy hadn't lit any warning signals in him.

Grace swung to him, halting his progress as he maneuvered behind her. A sneer smeared across her lips. "She's been with your brother. Did you know that?"

Shock nailed him in the solar plexus. His brother and Grace?

"She's been sneaking out to meet him, reporting about you." An evil, throaty laugh bubbled out of the demon. She stopped, her voice dropped low. "And do you know why? Your name should explain it."

He stilled. Grace knew his dirty history, but it felt like the ultimate betrayal the demon would use her to spill his secrets.

"Like she said, her birth parents are still alive...her *prime* birth parents. And you're just a former blood whore from the streets, Ozias Rourke."

Rourke ground his teeth down so hard he was astonished his fangs didn't poke out the other side of his lower lip. His eyes shot to Demetrius.

His friend's expression held only distrust for the creature. "I hate to insult you, demon, but I'm gonna go ahead and wait for proof about Grace's parents."

Grace held her arms out and glanced down at her body. "Is it not enough proof I'm here? She must be the one to say the words, after all."

There it was. Out there for everyone else to hear now—Rourke's main hang-up about this whole ordeal.

"Riiight." Demetrius cocked a brow. "Because demons are open and honest about their intentions. What, exactly, made Grace speak the vows?"

Grace glared back and forth between the both of them. Her black gaze rested back on Rourke, a cruel smile curving her lips. "All Osiris had to do was ask."

His hands curled into themselves, his nails biting into skin, but Demetrius words were not lost on him. "If she were to reject me because I'm a filthy street whore, then I fail to see how my brother would turn her head."

A moment of indecision passed through her expression. So, it wasn't as cut and dried as the demon purported it to be.

Shocker. He almost felt ashamed, but the truth was still out there, and he didn't know why Grace had betrayed them all.

"We're gonna go ahead and lock you up until we figure this out." Demetrius advanced on her.

She hissed at him and crouched to attack. The demon would do everything but destroy the body to get away.

Fast as lightening, Rourke lunged to wrap his arms around Grace to pin her arms to her torso. He was flung back as easily as the paper shreds littering the room.

Shock registered in Demetrius's face. Grace possessed normal strength and very little fighting skill as a vampire, but the demon obviously knew how to fight.

Rourke was back on his feet in seconds. He couldn't bring himself to hurt Grace, no matter the circumstances. He wouldn't allow the demon to brutalize Grace's body in order to escape.

The demon and his friend were locked in battle. Arms tearing at each other, Grace attempting to claw Demetrius's face off while he grappled with her limbs to pin her down. Calli stepped in the doorway to block Grace's exit.

Prime hosts were too hard to come by. That fact was the only solace Rourke had the demon wouldn't seek Grace's death to stay out of confinement. He circled around behind her again, prepared for her new fighting skill. Demetrius knew what he was doing and dropped low.

This time when Rourke grabbed her around the middle, locking down her arms, she twisted and writhed. Sharp teeth slammed into his arm.

Gritting his teeth against the pain, he decided more acute measures were required to subdue Grace. With her teeth tangled in the mess she'd made out of his flesh, he released his other hand. Propelled by his speed and all the strength he had to lend, he thumped her on the head.

She slumped forward unconscious and her teeth released.

Grateful one hit was all it took, he swooped her up. Guilt ate at him. She'd heal, he told himself. It was the best way.

Demetrius and Calli eyed him. He set his mouth and strode out of the office with his bundle.

He was fine.

The other two followed with their towline of tension. They were all prepared to take on Grace again if need be.

Fuck, he wanted the demon's name. Associating Grace's name with that abomination wasn't right. Didn't *feel* right.

"It wanted the tome." Calli's voice was introspective. "I've been through that thing at least ten times. It packs a lot of information, but nothing that will bring down the underworld. I could only wish."

They moved swiftly through the hallway, winding their way down to the holding cells Demetrius had built into the place. They'd never been used. Death was a common solution to many of their problems.

Demetrius, the consummate leader, ticked off duties for all of them. "Calli, comb through the book again. There's something in there they either don't want us to see or will be incredibly useful to them. Zoey reported the possible human contact point the demons are using. Before sunset, I'll take Bishop to shake him down."

Rourke cradled his rapidly healing arm and waited for his assignment with trepidation. He didn't want to leave Grace's side, but he was afraid Demetrius would order him to do so. Or he'd order Rourke to work another angle to this mess, and that was even worse.

"You gotta find out who her birth parents are, if they exist."

Hellfire. There was that. Researching prime families would've been fine before his past was dredged up to the forefront and thrown in his face in front of his team, his friends.

Demetrius continued, "Grace might be able to tell you when she comes to. Get anything you can out of her. When you do, we find them, we find your brother."

"That guy," Calli spoke up, "the cult leader, Terrance Walkins… He might know how to throw a demon out of a host."

Both males swung their gaze toward her, surprise etched in their features.

Genius.

"I mean," Calli shrugged, "if you deal in the business of hosts, my guess is you'd cover your ass by having a get out of jail free card. Have the upper hand, so to speak. Maybe that's what they don't want me to find," she mused, her brows drawn in.

Their assumptions had been pigeon-holed by their limited experience, which included beheading or staking a host and sending the demon back to the underworld.

Finally, they reached their destination. Grace's slight weight wasn't cumbersome, it was the conflict raging within. His instincts drove him to comfort her, watch over her, but he needed distance from her.

Demetrius opened all the doors. The cell was behind a triple locked door, in a room with a cage of double layered bulletproof Plexiglas reinforced with metal bars between the layers. Mostly see-through, and damn hard to break out of.

Cameras hung in each corner where Creed could watch her day and night.

Rourke almost growled.

He had to get over it fast. Writing Grace off completely wasn't on his agenda, but scribbling her out of his heart was. He couldn't with her. Just couldn't.

Because no matter what filth the demon spilled, Grace was still with his brother without telling him, and she hosted a demon. Those two items gave him the it's-you-and-not-me excuse.

He bent to lay Grace down on the cot. A very subtle stench of brimstone wafted off of her.

He dropped her the rest of the way and stalked out of the cell.

She groaned as the door clicked shut. Rourke stopped with his back to the cell. The intensity of his gaze could've set fire to the floor.

"Rourke?" Grace's hoarse whisper ripped the remnants of his resolve.

Steeling himself, he spun slowly around.

She was sitting up, rubbing her temples, when she paused to peer around. Her face drained of color and when her eyes met his, they were brimming with guilt.

"Talk." All of Rourke's disappointment poured into that one word.

"Rourke—"

"Don't." He pinned her with a dark glare. "Talk."

Her hands twisted in her lap, resembling what his insides looked like. His heart was having a difficult time carving her out of it.

She swallowed hard, her eyes dropping to her hands. "He caught me after I ran out of the club when Bishop was jumped. I was persuaded to go with him when he said my birth parents were still alive."

"You believed him?" His tone was flat. He was slowly winning the war to close his emotions back up in a box. Grace had made him feel, and it sucked as badly as he remembered.

"How could I walk away? I'd lost them all and when he said that, it was…" Tears welled in her eyes. She sniffled. "Anyway, he took me to this mansion. I can't tell you where it's at."

"How convenient."

"He showed me their picture," she said quietly, studying her hands.

"And?" If he appeared too interested, the demon would take over to prevent Grace from giving him details. He needed time with Grace to learn as much as he could about her "parents" and Osiris.

Hastily wiping her eyes, she gathered herself. "If they're fake, whoever chose them for the photo did a bang-up job. They looked like me."

Rourke ensured no spark of intrigue entered his dark gaze. He measured his bored look on her.

"I mean, I'm sure I'm shorter." She gave a half-hearted laugh. "Height seems to be a theme with vampires." A soft, wistful sigh escaped. "He said the murdered couple were my caregivers. He said you did it, said you killed all of them. He wants to frame you, and I don't know why."

Rourke didn't know either. He'd always been dispensable to his family, another mouth to feed when they couldn't afford it. For Osiris to hate him so severely he'd pursued him for decades to frame him for murder…Why?

They'd been street poor, so who was Osiris working for who had a mansion? Another prime family? If, by a long shot, the mansion was his brother's, what had he sold to get that much money?

A slow realization crept into Rourke.

Indeed. What *had* his brother sold?

"Osiris is possessed." He didn't ask. In his gut, he knew.

Grace's beautiful brown irises grew black until the demon took over with a menacing laugh. "You're not nearly as stupid as your brother claimed." She cocked her head at him, her gaze sweeping his body. "It's a shame the bond never took with you. You'd have been a worthy host, despite the circumstances of your birth."

Cold blanketed his insides at her revelation. Perhaps the demon was messing with him. He had no recollection of a bonding ritual.

"Yesss," Grace's demon squealed with glee. "The power in prime families' blood tolerates hosting one of the Circle better than commoners, yet…it was worth a shot. Your parents were deliciously greedy, so willing to turn over a good price for you."

"They did turn over a good price for me, only not to you." He'd had too many years of confinement and abuse to work through his emotions of why and wondering what he'd done to deserve any of it. The underworld wasn't going to play him.

The demon sat back, wearing a Cheshire grin. "Their ingenuity was impressive. You were broken, making our deal null and void. But they managed to put your other traits to use."

Blood and sex. What else was there?

The demon was still smiling, as if waiting for Rourke to ask and dammit, he had to. "Broken?"

If possible, the grin widened, transforming Grace's features into those that weren't her own. "Like Callista Augustus," the demon spit her name out, "we were going to bond you to a demon, only one from the Circle, one of *us*. A test, to see if it'd actually work with a commoner."

His mind spun over the data. Calli had been bonded to a second-tier demon so when she came of age, Draken could roam the earth freely. If he was bonded to a Circle demon, would that mean the demon could walk into his body when he came of age?

She waved her hand as if it wasn't a big deal. "You weren't strong enough. Obviously. You just weren't strong enough. I told them it wouldn't work."

"Then why try?" And how did it fail?

She shrugged and glanced away. Information the demon didn't want him to have? Prime families weren't as easy to target as they'd thought, so they went after commoners.

"You broke," she said finally, laying all the blame on his child self. "You're still broken, showing us how wrong it all was." Her eyes grew even darker. "At least you're not stupid like this one. She doesn't even know what you are to her."

His brows drew down. What could he be to Grace?

"Your bonding instinct's been busted since you were a child, but this *prime* girl can't even interpret her own feelings to know you're true mates."

Chapter Fifteen

Early the following night, Rourke addressed both Bishop and Demetrius as they were leaving the compound for their mission of hunting down the cult leader assisting the underworld. "I'm going with you."

The males didn't argue. That's why Rourke liked them. They knew if he hadn't gone back to Grace's cell, it was for a damn good reason and he'd explain on the way.

"Did you get any rest?" Demetrius asked.

"No." Rourke had spun out of the cell as soon the words "true mate" left Grace's mouth. He trusted Demetrius to assign Creed to monitoring the cell, and he stormed back to his apartment, his safe place.

How could he rest after his talk with the demon? Could he believe *any* of it?

Was it plausible? Yes. His family would've bartered him for top dollar, and if someone came offering thousands for their son's soul...well, easy answer. If that had failed and they could still get a good rate selling him to a blood slaver…well, he knew the answer.

His true mate would be a prime daughter? Impossible. No, Grace wasn't raised with a traditional prime family, but if those were her bloodlines, she'd be welcomed right back. With their fairly new medication bypassing the link and allowing true mates to share their bodies with others, Grace wouldn't have to stay with him. Why would she?

If he didn't have to be linked with *himself*, he wouldn't.

Oh wait, his link was broken.

"I need to feed from one of you." Rourke noted astonishment from Demetrius while Bishop paled. "At least try. D, you heard the demon claim they attempted the same with me that Calli went through, only with one of the thirteen. I might not have trouble feeding because either Grace isn't my true mate or my bonding instincts were destroyed. Or I'm one of those vampires where it doesn't matter. But if I do…"

Demetrius recovered first. "I'm offended Rourke. You don't want to try to have sex with me?"

Again, Rourke was impressed by Demetrius's relatability despite his prestigious background. "I don't want to offend Calli."

"Are you sure we shouldn't bring in Zoey or Ophelia for you to feed from?" Bishop rumbled, still looking less than thrilled with the idea.

Rourke shook his head. "If I can't feed from you, I can't feed from them. Gender won't matter to the mating bond."

Without hesitation, Demetrius raised his wrist. Bishop lifted his slowly, but noticed Demetrius beat him to it and dropped it with visible relief.

Well, I didn't want to sink my teeth into you either, big guy.

He grasped his friend's wrist and brought it to his mouth. The closer his mouth got to Demetrius's skin, the bigger his grimace grew.

Demetrius tensed, halting him. "You actually have to bite me. It's obvious you don't want to feed from me, but with Callista, I couldn't bear to swallow another's blood. As you well know," he growled.

Yes, he did recall plugging Demetrius's nose and mouth until he swallowed Zoey's life-saving blood. And he'd do it again, for any of them.

Exhaling, he stared down at Demetrius's wrist. His gut squirmed at the idea. Demetrius and Bishop stood as still as statues, waiting.

Snarling, he bared his fangs and struck. Demetrius flinched, but didn't pull his arm away.

Warm, rich blood filled Rourke's mouth, but it could've been raw sewage the way he reacted. He ripped his fangs away and heaved the tiny amount of blood onto the floor. Good thing he hadn't been up to eating breakfast earlier.

Coughing and retching, Rourke at least remained upright.

Demetrius's dry voice reached his ears. "Well, we have our answer."

"It can't be," Rourke rasped. He straightened to Demetrius closing the wound he had made.

Bishop scowled. "Why not? Grace is a solid female."

"She's prime." Rourke scrubbed his mouth and scanned his body. Wearing black had major advantages.

"You've been hanging out with me for forty years, and I'm prime," Demetrius pointed out.

"I work *for* you. It's different from being mated."

Demetrius studied him. "Is that why you've never mentioned your past? I mean, Rourke, I don't fucking care who gave birth to you. And as for what happened to you…" He blew out a gusty breath of disbelief. "…fuck man, we all have our skeletons and some are worse than others."

Bishop nodded the whole time. "We figured you'd been through some shit, but we respected your wishes to kept it to yourself. Because it doesn't matter."

Rourke heard their words, but in his soul, he couldn't believe him. Not when he'd grown up having it demonstrated how little he meant. The two males were prime, it was easy for them to say.

"You don't believe us." Demetrius started down the hall, expecting them to follow. "If you need another forty years for us to prove it, so be it, but we're wasting moonlight."

In an uncharacteristic move, Bishop clapped Rourke on the shoulder. "You're one of us, like it or not. Now let's go save your mate."

The male expected the best from Grace, assumed her reasons were sound for doing what she'd done. Yet after confirming her true mate status, Rourke could not. Her betrayal ran too deep.

Rourke walked behind them, deep in thought. He had an idea of how to find his brother, but they needed to deal with Grace's demon first. "D, Grace said she saw a picture of the couple who are supposed to be her parents. She said she looks like them."

His brow creased in thought, Demetrius punched a number on his phone. "It's me. Are you naked?" Bishop snorted. Demetrius passed the info along to Calli and pocketed his phone when he was done. "She's on it. Rather Ophelia will be since she knows prime families better."

Yes, she did. Their petite team member was pulling double agent duty, gathering intel on which prime families are playing host for the Circle. They were up to six.

Seven with Grace.

***

"So…this is the address." Demetrius eyed the quaint structure as dubiously as Rourke was.

They stood a block away from a colonial house painted seafoam green with cozy black shutters, a full porch, and stately columns.

"It's close to the university." Bishop untucked his shirt to cover the weapons strapped around his waist.

Rourke and Demetrius followed suit. This wasn't the neighborhood three heavily armed males stalked through after dark. This area was where children were snuggled into bed by ten p.m. and their parents watched the nightly news before turning in.

Demetrius assessed the property. "Freemont-U, a loaded recruiting ground for nubile young women shunning the world, forging their own way, and introduced into a world where supernatural is super-hot."

"I doubt it's just women," Rourke added.

"You're right, my friend." Demetrius stepped off the sidewalk to creep through the lawns until they reached their target. "Our cult leader may be an equal opportunity corrupter. It'd be the smart thing. Demons could shop through hosts like they were at a consignment store."

A small growl escaped Bishop. "The demons would use them mercilessly. They'd have no say over their bodies."

Stepping through lawn ornaments and bypassing motion lights, they ran into trouble two houses away.

A large, white poodle barked until it went hoarse.

The three of them crouched low in a row of brittle lilacs long past bloom, the majority of their leaves already fallen.

The backdoor to the house opened. "Simba, what the hell?" A woman in a bathrobe plucked on the leash. "The neighbors are going to call the police on us again."

Simba fought like hell, his eyes piercing the branches to where the three of them hid. The woman eventually won the tug of war, dragging the straining poodle inside.

"A dog that fancy shouldn't have a such a ferocious bark." Bishop stepped out of the branches.

They fanned out automatically, not having to consult each other. Rourke sucked in deep breaths, tasting the air. The faintest tang of brimstone hung on the breeze, but otherwise he detected no vampires or shifters.

He jumped the fence between the poodle's yard and the next and crept around the back of the house. It was two stories high with a basement. Rourke snuck up to the basement window to peer inside. He sensed Bishop and Demetrius doing the same to the rest of the windows.

Seeing nothing of consequence other than a dank basement used as storage, Rourke straightened. He stepped over landscaping rocks and turned the corner to find Bishop hanging off the roof of a wraparound porch to spy inside an upper level window.

For such a large male, he was stealthy as hell. Rourke marveled at the many positions he'd found his big friend in. If business with Demetrius ever got slow, Bishop could make a hell of a living as a cat burglar.

"Nothing." Bishop jumped down, landing lightly in the grass.

"Over here," Demetrius's whisper floated on the breeze.

Rourke never minded stalking humans. Their dull senses made for a cakewalk mission, exactly what Rourke needed right now.

He and Bishop found Demetrius staring into a first level window with dull glow emanating from it. All three dropped when the front door opened, their black clothing blending seamlessly into the shadows.

Giggles traveled through the night air. Two ladies sauntered down the front walk toward a large Jeep. One woman was dark and lanky and the other was blonde and curvy. Bishop stiffened next to him. Rourke glanced over to see Bishop's gaze riveted on the blonde. No wonder, the girl was right up Bishop's alley. Unfortunately, her association with this house marked her off Bishop's prospective list.

"I don't know." The brunette was speaking. "It seems so…unknown."

"That's the thrill of it. You don't know what you're going to get, or what's going to happen."

The breathless quality to the blonde's voice relayed her excitement. "When I was a host, I came to and my body was deliciously sore. The side of my neck was tender, like maybe a vampire drank from me."

Demetrius shook his head. Rourke's disbelief was as strong. Who the fuck would turn their body over for someone's use—*willingly?* How many years had he plotted and planned to gain his own freedom? Too fucking many.

Reason number one to butt this cult leader out of business: protect those who are too stupid to protect themselves. Someone else might think the girl deserved what she got, but to Rourke it was wrong. All of it was wrong.

The other girl shivered at the blonde's words. "You have no memory of what happens while they're…while you're…"

"I wish. I guess that's only for the powerful vampires." She fluffed her light hair. "I plan to become one someday."

Rourke exchanged a *wft?* look with Demetrius. So that's how this guy recruited them. The humans had no idea it was impossible.

"How many more times do you have to host?" The brunette's eyes were full of excited trepidation.

The curvy girl frowned. "I dunno. Terrance said it takes a lot, but each time the vampire essence builds within us, and with each vampire feeding, we start to change."

Bishop dropped his head down, like he gave up. Rourke commiserated. The lies were beyond believable, and that the guy responsible found vulnerable people to attract for the demons' use was inconceivable.

They had to protect the secrecy of their species, but it opened doors for all kinds of misinformation to get passed around in order to manipulate others.

And that's exactly what the demons were doing to vampires, how they recruited primes to possess.

The girls climbed into the vehicle and drove off. The three of them crouched in silence for a moment.

"Hellfire." Demetrius's voice was full of anger and disbelief. "No wonder the demons want to keep the tome out of our hands. They can con primes like they do humans."

"My thoughts exactly." Rourke straightened, while Bishop stared numbly at the grass.

His friend had a big heart, but Rourke was surprised how the humans' unwitting plight bothered the male.

Demetrius gestured to the window he'd been spying through. "Check out the view. A real B movie going on in there."

Rourke peered in. D's explanation was exceedingly accurate. "I'm surprised there isn't a guy with a black cape and fake fangs wandering around."

Candles rested randomly on every surface. A chandelier had been spray painted black and there was a large pentagram in the middle of the floor. A large table was pushed to the side, with a rug rolled up on top. They must cover up the demonic graffiti during the cult's off hours.

Bishop had risen and was staring through the pane next to Rourke. "I say it's time we pay this filth a visit."

Demetrius sniffed the air. "I can't sense well through the house, can't tell how many humans are inside, but we can't delay any longer. I don't think the girls locked up behind them. Whaddya say we go through the front door like the gentlemen we are?"

Rourke would never be accused of being a gentleman. "I'll take the back."

They broke off. Rourke circled to the back door and extracted a lock pick kit from his pocket. Some people carried wallets. Some people didn't need a wallet if they could pick locks.

The backdoor had a standard knob and deadbolt. In less than two minutes, Rourke pushed the door open. He heard no voices. Demetrius and Bishop hadn't encountered anyone yet.

Candlelight filtered through the rooms. Rourke exited the mud room into a kitchen. The floor above him creaked.

Demetrius whispered from the front entry, knowing Rourke's ears would pick up the sound when human hearing couldn't. "Clear the basement. We're heading upstairs."

After a short search, Rourke located the door to the basement. He swiftly combed the area. Two journals and a tub of occult materials containing candles, ugly statues of gargoyles, and sinister chalices caught his eye. The egress window was barely large enough for the tub, but he wrestled everything into the well outside. They'd grab it before they left.

No raised voices greeted Rourke as he ascended the stairs, nor when he cut through the living room to climb to the second level. He stepped cautiously to prevent any creaking, and when he reached the top, Demetrius and Bishop stood listening at a door at the end of the hall. Bishop held his phone to the door.

Demetrius held up three fingers, switched to two, and then only one. He bent the remaining finger until it was horizontal to the floor.

Three humans, two were standing and one was prone.

The closer Rourke got, the clearer the sounds of faint chanting were. A ritual was being performed, and Bishop was using his phone to record the words.

He pulled up next to the others to listen.

Latin?

He listened to the ancient language being spoken on the other side. Demetrius and Bishop probably understood, but he had never learned.

Demetrius moved his lips, barely any air passing through, but Rourke understood what he said. "The man is calling for the spirit. He's on his fifth time repeating it. Bet he's going for six, seems to be one of the underworld's pet numbers."

He nodded as if the sixth round had begun. They were caught between preventing another human being possessed and learning as much as they could to protect everyone. How far could they allow this ceremony to go? As long as they needed to help their people.

A groan resounded from the room.

A man Rourke figured was Terrance Walkins used his best ominous vice to ask, "Is this the one known as Stryke?"

Another hoarse voice answered, "It is I."

"How may we be of service?" One of the three was a woman.

"Is this the best body you could get?" the demon answered.

An awkward heartbeat passed before Terrance said, "I apologize if it does not fit your needs. I can hold you in this plane until nightfall. You will have to bond with a strong being in order to be able to cross freely."

"I know the drill," the demon grumbled.

Once they heard rustling inside like they were going to leave the room, Demetrius nodded to signal Rourke.

He backed up a few feet from the door. Demetrius and Bishop bordered each side of the door, weapons drawn.

Rourke might've trained himself to open any lock he came across, but nothing beat a solid kick.

He raised his leg and slammed his foot right above the door knob. Wood splintering was extremely satisfying as the door shuddered open.

A human man and woman, two people who could blend in almost anywhere in Freemont among decent people, stood with their mouth agape. A second human male, young and unfit, with soulless black eyes lay between them, his black gaze narrowed on the three vampires.

The woman recovered first, diving for a nightstand Rourke guessed held a weapon. The man who carried out the ceremony reached into his waistband for a silver gun. Rourke's opinion of him grew a notch. Only because the couple was smart enough not to bring a demon into the realm without a way to put the host down and send the demon back to Hell if things went sideways.

The possessed man laid a hand on the other man's chest, stalling him in his scramble for a weapon. The woman spun with her own gun raised, but the demon held his other hand up to halt any further action. Two small movements that showed his power over them.

Both Demetrius and Bishop had the humans in their sights, ready to fire to wound. Killing humans was much more complicated than other species. Police, paperwork, a trail of their existence, people who searched for them. It all got messy, as did wounding them, but it was easier than hiding a body.

The demon spoke first, addressing the humans. "Put your guns down, Terrance, Gail. You don't stand a chance against these males."

"I'm flattered." Demetrius's level tone was suspicious. "Our reputation precedes us. Perhaps, you'd like to introduce yourself...Stryke"

A deep chuckle that didn't fit the mouth of the marshmellowy male was pure demon. "Oh, I definitely know your reputation." His dark gaze studied them. "Bishop. Rourke."

Rourke's brow furrowed. There was familiarity in his voice. It was like Stryke knew them, not just heard of them.

The two humans who summoned Stryke shifted. Gail's hand was frozen around her pistol, the aim random, not pointed. Terrance's fingers were wedged between his back and his own weapon tucked into his waistband. They both watched Stryke, who searched behind Rourke and his team with a disappointed expression.

"Just you three. Damn." Stryke's disappointment was palpable. Which one of them did he want to see? He sighed. "What a wasted trip."

Questions ran through their heads at the demon's non-confrontational behavior when Stryke yanked Terrance to him, securing the gun in his own hand.

The three vampires lunged, but with speed the non-athletic male surely couldn't possess, Stryke shot Gail as he wrapped an arm around Terrance's neck. Terrance's eyes bulged before the gun was dropped, and Stryke used his free hand to jerk the man's neck up and sideways.

"No!" Rourke bellowed, lunging for Stryke.

Rourke's hopes for freeing Grace drained away with the human's life force. Terrance and Gail were their best source at finding a way to release Grace from her demon.

Rourke didn't realize his fangs were exposed. He'd prepared to rip out the human's throat to reach Stryke, prepared to exact revenge for destroying his chance at saving Grace. Solid hands wrapped around his biceps like a vice. Only one male had the strength to restrain Rourke.

"Let me go, Bishop." His eyes had to be blazing red from rage.

Rourke's gaze rebounded around the room. All the humans were on the ground. Demetrius was perched on top of Stryke, pinning him down. Terrance sprawled on the floor, his head at an awkward angel, while a red hole bloomed in the middle of Gail's forehead.

"You bastard." Rourke strained against Bishop's hold, but his words were for Stryke.

The demon remained lax under Demetrius, like he didn't have a care in the world. "I'm sorry, did you need to talk to them?" He spoke with supreme effort despite his relaxed expression.

"Without Terrance, he can't stay in the human." Demetrius gave the demon a little shake.

Rourke finally freed himself from Bishop and dropped to his knees by Stryke's head. Demetrius watched them both warily.

The smirk faded from the human's face as Rourke clutched the man's chin. "How do we release her?" He squeezed so hard, the human's face went pale from the pain. The demon might be able to tolerate a lot, but the host couldn't. "How?"

"Is that why you're here? They actually succeeded getting Bita into a host?" He fell silent, his breathing growing more labored. The demon was trying not to fall off the figurative cliff that led to Hell, hanging onto his host for dear life. "I'm sorry, Rourke. I truly am, but I couldn't have these humans spilling our secrets. Not until I get what I want."

"And what is that?" Demetrius asked, his pale green eyes blazing.

A lazy smile spread across the host's face. "Not a what, and nothing to do with what you're fighting. It's my business alone. Terrance and his wife can no longer answer your question. I'm afraid you'll have to go back home and read between the lines."

Rourke ripped his hand off the man's face in disgust. Demetrius fisted the collar of the human's dime store shirt and lifted him.

"What are we supposed to find?" His friend made one last attempt to extract information.

They were too late. Blackness drained from the male's eyes, revealing confused blue orbs that rolled back into the man's head before he passed out.

With a snort of disgust, Demetrius dropped his load.

"Sirens," Bishop announced. "The gunshot did not go unnoticed in this neighborhood."

Demetrius straightened. "Collect everything you can and flash back."

Rourke didn't plan to waste time. He flung open the window and removed the screen. "I found some items in the basement. I'll meet you back there."

He jumped, landing easily on the grass in the backyard. Demetrius and Bishop didn't touch the ground, flashing as soon as they had jumped.

People searched the neighborhood from their windows, he could sense it. They heard the gunshot, but didn't know if it was a car that backfired, kids messing around, or an actual gunshot. His sensitive sight picked out the humans living across the street watching this house. Most likely the ones who called the cops. The couple Stryke killed must've raised some red flags amongst their neighbors with various people coming and going at all hours of the night. Little did they know it wasn't a meth house in their midst. It was much worse and more dangerous.

He wrestled the items out of the deep window well and flashed back to the compound.

Chapter Sixteen

Rourke pressed his phone to his ear while he was crowded into Calli's office with Demetrius and Bishop. Papers still littered the floor, only now all the items Rourke had stolen lined the tables.

Calli sat hunched over the tome, making curt, frustrated noises as she flicked each page over. Any more force, and she'd rip the heavy parchment that constructed the book.

They'd found nothing to help Grace, and they all felt the pressure. How much more corruption was she exposed to the longer it took to rid her of the evil?

"She's demanding to talk to you." Creed's voice filtered through the line.

Rourke wanted to crush...everything around him. "*She* can wait."

Creed had called when the demoness Bita took over and demanded to speak to Rourke. From the insults being spewed, Bita only sought to provoke him into hating Grace. Grace's voice screamed through the speakers Creed used to listen in on the holding area. *Pathetic blood whore. Simple-minded vampire trash.*

Rourke disconnected after she shouted, "Your parents should've sold you as soon as you were born!" After Bita's rants, exposing his past wasn't limited to Demetrius and Bishop.

He wasn't stupid. The demon was trying to incite his hatred for Grace and dam any willingness to help save Grace.

Bita was wrong. He didn't hate Grace. He was disappointed in her. And that was much worse. His brother he hated. His parents he had grown to hate. All had disappointed him initially. The loss of trust in Rourke's world severed the ties of a relationship, any relationship.

"Rourke," a husky voice attached to a tiny vampire said.

He glanced up. Ophelia was in the doorway, measuring the tension in the room. Her sharp mind would piece together the answers to all her unspoken questions.

"I have news on the primes we've been looking for." She held out her own phone.

Those damn phones were almost more important than their guns. The display showed a clear shot of a bald man with the same gingerbread brown eyes Rourke used to love gazing into before they could turn black like oil.

He snatched the device and thumbed through Ophelia's surveillance photos.

Her parents were fucking grocery shopping. With a young male, about five years of age. An odd errand for a well to-do family.

It actually made sense. If they lost their last child when the babysitters got slaughtered, they probably didn't go anywhere without their young.

The boy resembled Grace. He'd be surprised if this wasn't her birth family. Her features were a perfect blend of the male and female in the photo.

"It's daylight. I came back to show you this. They'll be okay until tonight. D?" Ophelia's glittering gaze landed on Demetrius.

Demetrius grunted to let her know he was listening while he was bent over Calli's shoulder.

"Bring the Blanchettes in or watch them for another night?"

"I only know the name," Demetrius muttered. "That's a good sign."

"Exactly." The name echoed in Rourke's head.

A fine prime name. The lack of familiarity was a good sign. It meant the Blanchettes didn't frequent the social club where Rourke and his team had to ferret out information. They weren't involved in any problems Demetrius had been called to take care of. They were likely a good family.

A good prime family. No wonder Grace turned on him.

Demetrius rubbed his chin and straightened. "Go out as early as you can tolerate and bring them in. Tell them they're in danger, and you'll tell them why when they arrive here, blah, blah, blah."

"You want to be the one to spill the secret their long lost daughter is still alive but she's possessed. Got it." Ophelia perched on top of a long table. Confetti from Grace's last visit fluttered to the floor. She gave a low whistle. "Your honey did a bang up job in here, Rourke."

Automatically on the defense, he snapped, "It was Bita."

A perfectly formed eyebrow arched on her delicate face, but she turned her attention to Calli. "Good thing we scanned and backed up the files of all that shit last week, huh?"

"Very good." Calli's face had been scrunched in a perpetual frown all night. She sat back with a huff and massaged her temples. "I don't get what this thing is hiding. It gives us all kinds of details about conjuring demons. The various levels of demons and the Circle of Thirteen."

She slammed the book shut and slumped back in her chair. Demetrius's fingers kneaded her shoulders, his expression troubled he couldn't help his mate.

As Rourke's gaze lingered on them, a flare of jealousy ignited. It was nothing new. The ember of envy was what had gotten him into a fight with D in the first place all those years ago. Every so often it sparked because, dammit, Demetrius was the male Rourke wished he'd been born as.

Shaking off the self-pity and extinguishing the spark of emotion, Rourke turned his attention to their problem.

"It's like the diabolic creatures crafted the book so if it ever fell into the wrong hands, it would be full of conjuring information but not how to undo any of it. The tome is a shovel for us to dig a big ol' hole with."

"Run through what we do know." Ophelia picked at her nails. The female always appeared to be oblivious to her surroundings. It was pure deception, a second nature skill for her.

Calli opened the cover and flipped pages as she spoke. "The beginning is a who's who of the underworld, starting with the Circle. Like it says Bita is a nightmare demon and Malachim, the one who possessed my father, is the second in command in the Circle. They can inhabit a host, but don't ever use the bond to cross because what dies on earth stays on earth. Then there's the second tier demons like Draken..." Her lip curled in disgust and she shuddered. "...who can possess with limited access to their powers. Or, if the bond is strong enough, they can cross in their own forms. And they're humanoid, they blend. Inhumanly tall, horned, with atrocious fangs, Malachim would most definitely not have blended."

Demetrius filled in the rest. "The rest of the book is incantations to summon each demon. The ceremony to bond a host. All of it's useful, but not even the journals from Calli's mother mentioned an undoing."

Ophelia snorted as she filed her trim nails. "At least your mama wrote fluently and not the halting way the tome is written."

Rourke hadn't touched much of Calli's research. She had passed on what was important, and he had carried out the duties. But they were struggling, running into walls. He'd have to step up, no matter how inferior he felt compared to the other minds in the room.

He threw his few brain cells into the ring. "Did they have a different language or was it translated recently? Is that the reason for the odd writing?"

"No one knows," Calli answered. "It's like they weren't used to constructing paragraphs."

"Maybe they read differently." Rourke spoke before his good sense kicked in. He couldn't compete with Calli's intellect.

Calli's lips pursed and she scowled at the tome. Instantly, insecurity pierced Rourke.

Ophelia cocked her head, ruminating over Rourke's statement. "It's not like every society reads the way we do."

Calli slowly turned the pages until she reached the one with the bonding ritual. "The demon you called Stryke said 'read between the lines.' Perhaps he didn't mean it literally, but figuratively to read outside of the box. Although I still don't trust why he's helping us."

"They're tricky bastards." Demetrius peered over her shoulder. "He could be using us to betray the Circle, gain power, or some shit."

Rourke had been thinking on that since Stryke… "Stryke has to have an alternate method to gain access to this realm. If it were one of us, and you sent us to do a job, D, we wouldn't burn our only route to get it done."

Demetrius dipped his head in agreement. "The thought also crossed my mind."

"Chinese characters are read down and to the left. I'm not getting anything off that." Calli tilted her head. "Diagonally…nothing. Wait! There's a word."

Demetrius squinted at the letters, his head canted the same direction as Calli's. "How?"

Ophelia hopped down from the table and inched closer with Rourke, both of them unable to help themselves.

"Exactly opposite," Calli answered. "Up and to the right."

With her eyes glued on the page, her hand patted the desk, looking for a notepad and pen. She scrawled out each word as she interpreted the passage.

Rourke wasn't as familiar with the mating passage as Demetrius and Calli, obviously. Mated couples reported just knowing the phrase when they intended to carry out the ritual. It wasn't something widely shared. Nothing scared a single vampire more than being accidently mated. They were sexual beings, and while many secretly yearned to settle with their true mate, spending eternity with just one person terrified many of them.

It spurred the creation of the vampire version of the little blue pill. Circumvent the bond so they could have sex outside of the union. Have the urge to drink from another without symptoms of nausea.

While some could anyway, Rourke recalled his experience with Demetrius and tapping a vein that wasn't from Grace.

Apparently, his ability to bond wasn't as broken as Bita claimed.

"Rourke." Demetrius's voice busted through his retrospection.

Tearing his thoughts away from Grace wasn't easy. His mind was hung up on the bond and Grace.

His mind had to get the fuck over it.

"Before we evict Bita from Grace's body, go down and find out what she'll reveal."

Rourke's expression remained stoic, but a groan hovered at the base of his throat. It was a special kind of torture facing the demon in Grace's body. "Got it, D."

The long walk down to the holding cell took forever, but was much too fast for Rourke's taste. He stopped at Creed's man cave and knocked on the door.

"'Bout time." Creed sat on his ergonomic exercise ball chair. *Keeps the abs tight*, he argued when Rourke had spotted him carting it through the hallway.

It went with Creed's personality is what it did. Like the acceptable recyclable materials flyer he had made for all of them to hang above their trash cans. If he ever showed up to a fight in Birkenstocks, Demetrius had threatened to ship his blond ass off to Seattle.

An empty threat since Creed had five pairs.

"*Rourke*." the demon screamed in a ragged voice.

Grace's heightened awareness to his presence must've tipped Bita off.

"And she's back." Creed glanced at Rourke. "After you hung up on me, she screamed for a minute and then slunk back. Safe to say, Grace has a sore throat after all that yelling. Bita, though. That demon has some creative insults."

"They were accurate." Rourke got that out of the way, and he was actually comfortable confirming the demon's claims to Creed.

Of all his team, the male would understand being an outcast compared to the primes. Rourke didn't know the whole story, just that Creed was estranged from his parents.

"Yeah. I was gonna joke I'd trade childhoods with you, but I'll pass. You win." Creed swiveled back to the chess game on his tablet. "Go on in. D texted before you got here to have me record everything. So don't gush about the favorite lingerie you like on Grace."

The image of Grace's curvy body wearing nothing but lace and straps slammed into him. Lust flamed through his body, an arousal so forceful he was nearly driven to his knees. He spun out of the office, but didn't enter the holding room. The inferno inside of him would give him an instant disadvantage.

Steady breaths, the reminder of Grace's secret meetings with his brother, and Rourke was composed enough to enter.

"Weeelll," drawled Bita.

A name aided in separating Grace from the demon. Rourke should be grateful, but it was easier to distance himself from the female he'd allowed past his personal walls when he didn't know Bita's name. The line between Grace's victim status and betrayer stamp was clearer.

"You asked for me?" He held his gaze impassive.

Bita reclined back, a nasty smile on Grace's lush lips. "Was that a snarky comment from you? What more proof do I need that this weak female got under your skin?"

It was true. No reason to hide it anymore. If he didn't try, then it couldn't be used against him. Grace had affected him. Deeply. It didn't mean he was going to act the besotted male and become a target for the demon's machinations. Or his brother's.

Yet, his expression was a poster for boredom. "What'd you want." *By the way, demon hag, prepare to go back to Hell*.

Her stare turned calculating. "We're mates."

A snort of derision escaped him. "*You're* a demon, and wasn't it you who claimed my bonding sense was broken?"

"This Grace seems to feel for you." White fangs glinted past Grace's lips, her pink tongue flicked against them.

"You're hungry?"

She shrugged. "This female's tolerance for continuous healing is low."

Rourke scanned Grace's curvy body, keeping it clinical. Recovering from the fight with him and Demetrius, then Bita's epic tantrums, had taxed Grace. Dark circles ringed under her eyes and there was a slump to her shoulders that normally wasn't there. It was possible the constant internal battle drained her energy, required a higher level of replenishment than a natural bond.

He raised his gaze to meet her black one. "And you need my blood."

"I would think you'd want to keep your mate healthy."

"You said a prime daughter like Grace wanted nothing to do with me."

A mischievous smile twisted her lips. "She wouldn't if she was smart, but she seems to have a...*thing*...for you." Bita spit the word like any positive affection was weakness.

Rourke would agree with her. "You also said she betrayed me for my brother."

"You two can share her. I don't mind."

A shudder vibrated its way down Rourke's spine.

Bita let out a caustic laugh. "Your sexual stamina and his money. Together, you two are the perfect male."

Except for the circumstances of their birth. Less worth than commoners.

Regardless, he didn't know when Demetrius would arrive and he hadn't gleaned any information from the tricky demon.

"What happens to the underworld when its ruling body roams the earth?" He chose the route of picking at Bita's pride. "Trading one power zone for another?"

"No. Peasant." Her eyelids moved like she rolled her eyes, but the complete blackness made it hard to tell. "Our strength is not limited like all the species roaming the earth."

Said the demons who won't completely bond because they could get killed in this realm. Rourke lifted an eyebrow.

She settled back to assess him. "You really are handsome. I'll grudgingly accept the appeal, even with your station. You're a strong male, and…" Her gaze swept his body. "…easy on the eyes. Anyway, it only takes one of us in the underworld to maintain rule."

"Then why are there thirteen of you?"

"Because that's how many of us were spawned." She laughed like it was a hell of a joke. "Symbolism has power, and the number thirteen holds much significance, both above and below the human realm."

"Won't your rule slip away once the entire Circle finds a host?"

Grace's chin tilted up. He'd delivered a solid blow to her pride.

"Then we can pass back and forth freely. I'm sure you were told as much by the second tier failure who bonded to that Augustus child."

Calli. "Draken?"

"Mmm." A reluctant confirmation.

His phone buzzed with a text. Extracting it from his pocket, he read the message. Demetrius was on his way, and Rourke had gotten little information.

"Perhaps you shouldn't have targeted a child," he murmured, staring at his screen as if he'd absently said the words.

"Please," she scoffed. "It's ingenious. Grace should've been ours, but Osiris couldn't find the little brat. It cost him severely. He wouldn't have needed her if you hadn't been such a disappointment. Added to his reasons of why he hates you."

"As if he has any legitimate claim to despise me."

"He and your parents were promised riches, but you were a failure and Osiris stayed destitute."

"What payoff did I block? I heard he lives in a mansion."

"The one he's going to receive now that we have Grace." A condescending chuckle escaped.

"You vampires are like humans with your obsession with money."

"So you plan to dwell like a commoner when you inhabit this realm?"

"Ha! You're a funny one."

Nothing he'd been accused of before, but it proved demons weren't just after the blood power of the primes.

"Where's the boy?"

Bita frowned. "What boy?"

As if she didn't know. "The one who was taken when Osiris destroyed the last family."

Her expression was perplexed. "A prime child?" she asked hopefully.

A simple cut of his head to the left answered her question.

Her confusion remained. "Then why would I care? We learned our lesson with you. Perhaps the boy will follow the same path you took at a young age."

"The demon inhabiting Osiris isn't one of the thirteen?"

A flicker in her dark gaze disappeared before Rourke could discern what it meant.

"Why would you think we would target him when you were such a disappointment?"

Because Osiris was older, and would've been stronger at the time.

Bita's gaze flickered over his shoulder when the door opened. He didn't turn when Demetrius and Calli entered the room. Ophelia hung outside.

Creed remained in his office, but the scents of Zoey and Bishop lingered by the door.

All hands on deck for this case.

Demetrius flanked him on his right, while Calli took up a stance on his left. A current of alarm snaked through the oily orbs from which Bita studied them. Calli held a sheet of paper with what Rourke assumed were the words to the undoing written on it.

Bita's eyes flicked from the paper, to each one of them and back to the paper.

The sheet appeared in front of him, held by Calli who hadn't taken her eyes off of Bita.

The slightest smug curl on Grace's mouth made Rourke pause. Inspecting her closely, he passed the page to Demetrius who stood on his left.

The expression dropped and creases of tension appeared around Grace's eyes.

Demetrius snagged the sheet with a slight questioning look.

"You have the blood and the power to do this," Rourke explained.

"You're Grace's mate." Demetrius retained the paper, but steadied his attention on Bita.

Her jaw tightened imperceptibly when her eyes darted from the undoing to Rourke.

"I am, but as Bita liked to point out, I'm broken." The edge of Rourke's mouth lifted in a smirk.

Bita bared her fangs and colored drained from Grace's features. She lunged up and rammed the glass so hard Rourke flinched, as did Calli and Demetrius.

"Start reading," Calli urged.

Demetrius's voice filled the room. Bita rammed the glass over and over. Rourke's muscles vibrated. The urge to race to Grace's aid before the demon beat her unconscious was overpowering. He shoved his hands in his pockets, then snatched them back out lest he palm his lock pick kit.

Her screaming started as Demetrius reached the end of the passage. Rourke wanted to steal a glance and see how many more fucking words were left, but he couldn't pry his eyes off of Grace.

Blood streamed down her face. Each jolt against the Plexiglas opening a head gash even farther. Her nose was probably broken. He blanched at the sickening crack of more facial bones breaking. Reinforced as it was, the panel quivered with each full body blow.

Hellfire, wasn't this done yet?

When the black receded and a gleam of gingerbread brown flickered, Rourke jumped to the lock.

"Rourke, no!" Calli tugged on his arm, but he shook her off.

Both of them froze when Grace arched her back, her mouth frozen in a silent scream. Her arms were outstretched, rigid.

Rourke's kit was in his hand in a heartbeat, and he blindly chose any pick. He jammed it into the lock only to realize two things. One, he'd busted the slim strip of silver in half. Two, this lock was electronic and he fucking knew that, but Grace's agony zapped his mind.

Creed must've been on the ball in the control room because a click sounded before Demetrius intoned the last word and the shriek broke free from Grace.

Rourke kicked the door open the rest of the way only to pull up short. Calli bumped into him and gasped.

Grace was levitating, her back curved at an ungodly angle while she thrashed against some unseen force.

With one final, eardrum shattering wail, Grace collapsed to the ground. Her head hit the concrete floor with an appalling crack.

He and Calli lunged forward, but they were both snapped back.

"No." Demetrius's grip was an iron band. "I've seen this before. Stay back until the underworld claims Bita."

A gaping, black hole opened under Grace's body. An image of a horned biped beast rose from her body. Bita snarled and snapped at the unseen force pulling her from her host.

"She will always have a part of me." Bita snarled, her real voice grating and hoarse. "I will get her back."

The demon was dragged into the blackness.

Was that a real portal between realms? The yawning chasm rapidly shrunk, creating a suction.

Grace's body shifted, drawn toward the ingesting hole.

Rourke ripped his arm free from Demetrius and dove for her, wrapping his hand around her ankles. There was no gentleness, just a sense to get her the fuck out of there.

There was a slight resistance, a tug of war for Grace.

Then, the spot snapped closed, releasing shock waves that toppled everyone who stood on their feet.

Three vampires hit the ground. Grace's legs dropped like lead. Sudden silence.

Rourke blinked, his focus returning to the destroyed body in front of him.

***

Grace groaned and attempted to roll over, but her head *throbbed*.

What the hell had happened? Her memory was nonexistent. Slowly, her senses fed her information.

The delicious smoky smell warmed her and lessened the pounding. Had Rourke actually stayed the day? That'd be a huge development in their relationship.

Then Calli's scent and the one she learned was Ophelia wafted over her. Well, they certainly hadn't had a slumber party.

She pried her eyes open. Her blurry vision landed on a hunched form sitting in the chair across from her bed.

"Rourke?" she croaked.

God, he looked good. His head hung down between his broad shoulders, his hands folded, elbows resting on his knees. He hadn't moved.

She sat up with a gasp, then clutched her head as all the details rolled back.

The words Osiris coerced out of her. The slimy sensation that had oozed into her and taken control whenever it goddamn felt like it.

"Rourke, I'm so sorry." Her face screwed up with remorse. A sob escaped.

One clear memory was the coldness that had settled back over him. He'd closed himself off from her again.

"Save the apologies." His tone said they were unwelcome. "They're useless. Recover. We need you to find my brother, and maybe there's still hope we can find the boy before he's killed or defiled."

His voice was made of stone. But by now, she was in tune with him enough to detect the current of hurt and anger.

She'd cut him deeply, but she'd been trying to protect an innocent couple. Osiris would've hurt them to get to her, birth parents or not.

"My parents—"

"Are waiting in the conference room." A thread of bitterness this time. "Demetrius gave them the details. They lost a little girl at the same time you were orphaned. The Blanchettes look like you."

Blanchette. Her given name. A good one, though giving up Otto wasn't something she was ready to do.

He rose, his large frame looming over her. Where it should be comforting, welcoming, and if she had her way, it would be. Instead, it was disheartening. The barrier he'd built between them was more solid than any of the concrete structures comprising the compound.

She opened her mouth to say his name again, to plead with him to understand, but she shut it. Cleaning up this mess might be the only way he'd open back up to her. He had to know she'd easily sacrifice herself for a child or to prevent anyone else from getting hurt. At least in her parent's case, it had worked. The boy, though...

Rourke stalked to the door where he paused to glance over his shoulder. "You'll need to feed. Ophelia has offered. If you still feel a bond toward me, she has medicine for that."

Her jaw dropped. "What? Why?" She shook her head at his chilled stare, and immediately regretted the movement when the pain roared back. "You're just throwing us away? Do you even know the circumstances?"

"You collaborated with Osiris at my expense to save your prime parents."

He spoke with keen scorn that cut deep.

"And you don't think I should've tried to save them and the boy, Ari, and gathered as many details as I could to bring back to you? I trusted you could handle him if he went after you."

He turned to face her, his eyes as dark as any demon's. "That's the thing Grace. You didn't trust me or any of us. You found out the roots of your heritage and suddenly we became disposable."

How could he think that? She didn't have time to ask. He stalked out and the door to her bedroom slammed before her question finished forming.

Muted voices drifted in from the living area in her suite. No wonder she scented the other females.

Grace heard the front door open and close and the bereft feeling she was left with meant Rourke had left.

Ophelia charged in, her expression almost as cold as Rourke's. "Okay, let's do this." She flicked a small object toward Grace.

An oval capsule landed in her lap. She picked it up to inspect it, sniffing it delicately. The strong herbal odor crinkled her nose. It was the medicine to help her feed and not get sick.

"Excuse me." Grace held the pill out, away from her nose. "I'm not taking this."

"You need to feed and lead us to Osiris." The attitude coming from the little female wasn't sitting well with Grace. "That is, if you're not going to protect him."

If they all were going to treat her like last week's garbage, she didn't need to stay here. She had a family now—again.

All the determined words wouldn't change her heart breaking at how easily Rourke walked away from her.

Grace tossed the pill back to Ophelia, who snapped it out of the air with a glare.

"I'm not taking it, and I don't need your charity blood."

"It's not charity." Ophelia's voice rose. They were instant adversaries. "It's necessity. You've been to Osiris's place. You can flash there again. Are you strong enough to flash?"

Grace gave a stubborn shake of her pounding head.

"Are you unwilling to bring us to Osiris so we can kill him?"

"Of course not," Grace snapped. "Maybe I made an error in judgement. But excuse me if I'm a little annoyed Rourke's thinks I threw him to the wolves when I was the one a demon played house in."

"The wolves are the good guys in our world. You tossed Rourke to the side like his parents did. He thinks none of us knew, but I have friends in low places. I've heard all the sordid details."

"How? How in the world does he see it like that?" *I'm nothing like his parents.* Grace had been through hell. No. Hell had gone through her. Her soul withered like it'd been defiled—because it had.

"You didn't trust him when he clearly let his guard down and trusted you."

Grace exhaled, frustrated. "I was protecting him. I love him."

Ophelia's expression said *please*. "You say that now, after the damage is done."

Right. Grace hadn't told him before, but it's not like he was on his knees professing his everlasting love.

"Whatever. This argument needs to be with Rourke, not that getting him to stay in the same room with me so we can have it out will happen."

The other female's lips twitched, as if she wholehearted agreed and Grace rose a few notches in her opinion because of it.

Ophelia bit into her wrist. The tang of blood filled the air. Grace's fangs throbbed, she was famished. With great effort, she held her fangs in check while she drank Ophelia's powerful blood. Sinking them into the other female's flesh smacked of betrayal although it wasn't.

Eventually, the difficulty lessened to match what it had been like supping from her family. Grace sensed the same confusion from the tiny female as she felt herself. Only hers was slowly turning to horror.

She finished, and Ophelia snatched her wrist back.

"Oh my god." Grace wiped her mouth. "Shouldn't that have made me sick?"

"Not necessarily." When Grace glanced at her with skepticism, she asked, "Were you able to feed from anyone else after you met Rourke?"

Grace shook her head, her gaze dropping to the floor.

"Oh."

Yeah. Oh. "Are we not true mates anymore?" She might have just met Rourke, but she'd fallen hard. If they hadn't been mates since she woke up, it didn't lessen her feelings any. She was mad for the male and mad at him.

Ophelia scoffed. "That's never happened. True mates are together for life. Even when they circumvent our nature and step outside of their union, they're still stuck as mates."

"Has any of them had a demon exorcised from them?" The lack of a response was enough of an answer. "It's a bad sign, isn't it? Is Bita still in me?"

"Nooo. That bitch got a one-way ticket back to Hell." Ophelia's mouth quirked, like she had more to say.

"Tell me."

Indecision flashed through Ophelia's expression.

"Tell. Me." Grace would not accept anything less than the truth.

Ophelia cocked a delicate brow at Grace's demand. "Bita said she'd always be with you, and she'd get you back. Bita claimed Rourke broke after a failed bonding attempt. Perhaps it's something similar."

Quick to defend him, she said, "Rourke's not broken, he's just a dick." He *was* a dick.

He was a boy who'd been abandoned to a horrible fate and protected himself ever since. And he'd opened up with her. He'd even smiled with his eyes—just for her.

Ophelia calmly observed Grace's inner turmoil.

"He's not broken and neither am I." If Grace said it a hundred more times, she might actually believe it. Because the way she had spewed the human's blood all over his shoes, and turned green at Osiris's offer to drink from him, she was having a hard time convincing herself she suffered no lingering effects from Bita.

***

Rourke clenched and unclenched his fists. He stood outside the compound with Bishop while they both waited for Grace and Ophelia.

"What would you have done?" Bishop asked.

Rourke didn't have to clarify. They were all caught in the undertow of Grace's charm, like Rourke had been.

"I would've reported to Demetrius immediately."

His friend snorted. "Yeah. *You* would've. The rest of us may have, too. But…"

A glance at his friend revealed indecision in his eyes, troubled lines at his mouth. For the umpteenth time in weeks, he wondered if Bishop was okay.

"It's just…" Bishop shrugged as if struggling to find the words to explain his pensive expression, "There's a point we all think we can handle it. Our loyalty is with the team, but we think 'I got this,' when we may be in over our heads."

The blond giant's sincerity sliced through Rourke's distrust.

"I don't know Grace well, but I buried her family," Bishop continued. "The same family who rescued her when they thought she had no one. Both times she was helpless, but your piece of shit brother laid out a plan that gave her the illusion she had a modicum of power. Maybe it wasn't about whose bloodline came from where, but about who she could finally save."

Rourke swallowed the lump that had formed in his throat and threatened to split his trachea. He coughed back the unwanted feeling surging forward.

Hope. What a fucking joke of an emotion. How long had he held onto hope and no one had come to save him? He'd been a *child*. As an adult, he'd worked for everything he had. Earned it. No more hoping or relying on anyone.

Is that what Grace had felt? She mistakenly hoped to finally steer her circumstances instead of being driven off a cliff by them?

"Hey, boys." Ophelia shoved the door open, not bothering to hold it for Grace.

His should-be mate barged out behind Ophelia, but her features only registered mild annoyance.

Her cheeks radiated a pink glow, her body was mended, but the underlying pallor concerned him.

"Once y'all finish this search and destroy, we have some shit we need to cover." Ophelia rolled her eyes toward Grace, who avoided eye contact with any of them. "With my undercover gig, I have to sit this one out, but Creed gets to go and play."

As if summoned, Creed stepped out into the night.

Rourke wanted answers as to what Ophelia referred to, but Grace spoke first, her voice soft but strong. "How does this work?"

"I can follow your flash," he replied, ignoring the warmth infusing him just by speaking to her. "Bishop and Creed will hang on for the ride."

Her nod lacked any confidence. "Okay. Ready?"

He had the urge to reassure her, but he only said, "Ready."

She closed her eyes, likely to visualize the place. Bishop and Creed each laid a hand on his shoulder and buried their fingers into his flesh to anchor themselves for the ride.

Rourke tensed, and as soon as Grace disappeared, he followed.

There was a slight lag before he arrived standing in front of her like when they'd left. Towing nearly five hundred pounds of meathead slowed him down.

Grace's solemn gaze rested on a mansion.

"Whoa," Bishop chuffed. "That's obnoxious even for a prime."

"My family's place is bigger." Creed wasn't boasting. It was more like he admitted a shameful secret.

Grace's eyes narrowed on the place like she had x-ray vision. "His office can be accessed through the front door. It wasn't locked when he brought me here. Go in, and it's at the end of the left wing."

Bishop ran his hands over his weapons for one last self-check before they entered. "Good. If he's in there, he hasn't sensed us. That place is massive, we can infiltrate before he realizes what's going on."

"Go in the trees, Grace," Rourke ordered. "Wait for us."

"Like hell, I'm going in." Her light brown irises reflected her determination. She wanted revenge. Her negative reaction to Osiris was pleasing, at least.

Creed tapped her shoulder in a placating gesture that curled Rourke's lip—a mate's reaction to another male touching his female. "Do you have gun?"

Her fierce expression drained. "No."

"Knives, daggers, blades of any sort?"

"No."

"Wooden stakes?" Her glare should've skewered Creed, but he only smiled his signature friendly grin. "Then you see why we want you to wait outside."

"Osiris was alone each time he met me."

Stubborn female. Rourke pointed out information that hadn't occurred to her. "He didn't do all the killings by himself."

She sighed in defeat. "Fine." Her gaze captured his. "Be careful. I might be annoyed with you, but I don't want to see you hurt. Not that anything could get to you."

While her last statement was steeped in bitterness, her concern for him was apparent. For him. His team never worried about him—he was Rourke. But Grace was.

Maybe it wasn't about whose bloodline came from where, but about who she could finally save.

Chapter Seventeen

The males surrounded the front door. Creed checked for security wires and shook his head. They were clear.

Getting into regular locks was Rourke's specialty, and he was highly disappointed. The door pushed easily open.

Each of them had a gun drawn as they crept inside. Rourke was reassured by the short stakes secured to his thighs. They didn't make the best weapon, required a direct hit most vampires were too wily for. But tonight, their target was his brother's black heart. Rourke would ensure the shot.

Not a single light was on, but they sensed at least five other vampires. Brimstone clogged the atmosphere within the ornate mausoleum.

"Gentlemen," a male called from the upper level bannister, "we didn't order any take out, but it sure is appreciated."

Shadows moved above and below them. Five against three, and they still hadn't found Osiris.

"We've got this." Bishop's lips hardly moved so the attackers wouldn't hear.

Creed fired the first shot. No more posturing, they needed the fight to start so Rourke could break away.

It worked beautifully. The five males jumped them at once, one male aimed for Rourke.

Rourke holstered his gun and pulled a dagger into each hand. The attacker spun in with incredible speed. Rourke held his ground until the male was close enough. His fist shot out, catching the attacker off guard. Knuckles connected with cheekbone and the male flew back. Rourke yanked a stake free from behind him and landed on top of the thug, nailing him in the chest. Before the pile of dust formed beneath him, Rourke was up and racing down a long hallway.

It was a shame his attacker perished so quickly, but it worked in Rourke's favor. Bishop and Creed wouldn't be long. The five vampires—now four— they faced were too used to exerting their strength over those who were weaker. Rourke and his team hadn't coasted through their fighting life like that.

He located the office Grace had mentioned. Barging in, he smelled his brother under the layer of sulfur woven through the room. But Osiris was gone.

Rourke inhaled deeply. The scent was so strong, his brother must've just left.

The coward. Sensed the presence of justice coming for him and jetted, leaving his lackeys to take the fall.

Sounds of fighting had diminished by the time Rourke stalked out of the office.

Creed waited at the end of the hall. "Anything?"

"Just left." Rourke systematically searched every other room off the hall. With Creed's help, they finished in seconds.

"Bishop's taking the upper level." Creed jogged through the main floor. "Nothing."

Bishop leapt over the bannister to land soundlessly on the marble floor. "All clear. They may have an escape route from the underground level."

Rourke kicked one of the ash piles at his feet. Not nearly as satisfying as a body, but less blood all over his clothing. "Osiris wouldn't go there, unless it was to escape."

Creed wandered to a china cabinet and traced his fingers along the ornate detailing on the front. "If he ran, where would he go?"

Rourke's brow creased in thought. "Our childhood home is out of the question." Was there anyone he would—fuck. "*Grace*."

***

They're inside. Grace's stomach flipped, and she hopped from one foot to the other. Ophelia's blood was the equivalent of guzzling two energy drinks within minutes. How did her kind do this their whole life? No wonder vampires were long and lean. They must never quit moving. Then Grace remembered all the sex. Yeah, made sense. She had chalked it up to the excitement of first love with Rourke, but feeding from him charged her sex drive batteries.

A sigh escaped. Rourke. He'd actually seemed to warm to her a little earlier, not quite the cold shoulder she got when she'd come to after the demon extraction.

Settling into a crouch when she heard voices, Grace scanned the vast expanse of the lawn. The night was partially cloudy and it'd been two weeks since a full moon. Lighting wasn't the best, but Grace's vision made out the open front door.

The noise of fighting reached her ears. She hated hiding in the trees to protect herself, but she grudgingly accepted they had been right. The reality of them engaging in fights to the death drove home the fact she would've been nothing but a liability.

Would Ari be inside? During all of her own drama, he'd been gone, helpless. At the mercy of a ruthless male motivated by selfishness to aid the underworld. And Ari was three-years-old. Not much defense against Osiris.

A stick cracked on her left.

She rose and spun to face glimmering dark eyes.

"Osiris."

He drew in a full breath, his nostrils flaring wide. His face lost a few shades of color and his eyes grew wide. "Where's Bita?"

"Oh, you noticed I quit using my brimstone perfume?" Tonight, her shortage of a verbal filter would be her best asset or her biggest disadvantage.

She had no idea what Osiris planned for her now, but the guys were bound to return soon. Keep him talking.

"Impossible." His expression was full of disbelief. He sucked in more air to double check. "Fucking impossible."

"Seriously, it's not. Want to know how?"

Black bled into his eyes. The demon inside of him disliked her offer. Damn her mouth.

"Well, I don't know them. Bita hogged my body," she rushed out. Totally true. Grace had no memory of when the demon took over, and she hoped the demon bought it hard when the incantation was read.

His eyes faded back to his normal brown. Grace exhaled in relief. Her last confrontation with Osiris's demon was a horror movie come to life. Sad that "just Osiris" was a more desirable situation.

"Then Bita saved your life. If you had heard the words spoken to exorcise her, you'd be targeted for death." Osiris's gaze turned calculating. "However, you're still useful."

She took a step back. He prowled forward. She hastily backed up until she was clear of the trees.

"Grace." Rourke's voice echoed through the night. She spun to see him sprinting across the lawn with a look of sheer terror. Bishop and Creed exited the mansion after him.

An arm wrapped around her throat. Osiris yanked her against his hard body. She threw her elbows back, but she might as well have been hitting a sheet of plywood. His other arm banded around her waist. She stomped on his feet, kicked his shins, until he tightened his hold around her neck and cut off her air.

"Stop," he ordered Rourke.

Rourke zeroed in on her face, noticing she struggled for air. He pulled up short, holding a hand up to stop Bishop and Creed behind him.

"Ozias." Osiris had an unreadable tone. His grip loosened, and she gulped in oxygen.

Grace expected hate, distain from Osiris for Rourke. His muscles vibrated with an unidentified emotion. She didn't know if it was a good sign or bad.

"Osiris." Rourke's eyes were glued to Osiris's. "Why Grace?"

"The Circle will either want her dead for being a vessel fail for Bita or use her again." He shrugged, momentarily closing off her air supply as he did. "She said the vows once; she'll say them again."

The idea sent a tremor through Grace. Hosting Bita again, losing her body to an evil entity... "I won't."

"All the threats still apply." He sounded so sure, so smug.

Rourke's gaze narrowed. "We have her parents. You've killed everyone else around her."

With sickening dread, Grace realized the trump card Osiris held.

Osiris grinned against her hair. "The boy."

Not Ari. So many had suffered because they wanted her, but Ari was by far the youngest and most innocent.

Rourke tilted his head as if considering the validity of Osiris's statement. His expression filled with disgust. "Why would you still have him?"

"Not for the reason you think. Sorry to disappoint you brother. I don't do that to children."

A snort and an eye roll escaped Rourke. Apparently, Grace wasn't the only one to squeeze emotion out of him. "But you stand by while it's done to them."

Osiris's intense energy faded into stillness. "You forget Ozias, life wasn't kind to me, either. Why do you think I wanted the money so badly? To share with parents who viewed children as an inconvenience and a resource to utilize?" He gave an indignant huff. "I used your misfortune to get myself out of there."

Rourke nodded, like Osiris's words confirmed something. "You killed them."

Fear shot through Grace. The brothers' parents were awful people, but if Osiris had been a minor, he'd started his killing spree early.

~273~

Osiris laughed darkly. "Want to thank me?"

"Was it before or after you sold your soul?"

"Touché, brother. After. Unfortunately, our dear mother and father kept me too weak to fight back."

"Let me guess how it played out. After they tried with me, whatever demon involved noticed you were older and more desperate to escape. The demons cut a deal. You get riches, and they'll help you gain freedom if you host."

"Bingo." Osiris sighed dramatically. "This conversation is getting boring—"

"Was there any time you thought to go after your twelve-year-old little brother who'd been sold as a blood slave?" Rourke's voice was quiet, laced with sorrow. Grace's heart cracked. He was a grown male, but a part of him was still the young boy who harbored a spark of hope that at least his brother might help him.

Staggering grief poured out of Osiris. "There was a time when I wasn't a heartless bastard, Ozias. And that was right after I gained freedom and was forced to grow strapping and healthy for the demon to enter me. It was clear where my road led. I couldn't take you on it."

"Keep telling yourself that." Rourke's look of derision hit Osiris hard. He went rigid behind her.

"You should *thank* me," he said between clenched teeth. "You would've never met Grace if I hadn't let those humans find her."

Grace twisted in shock to see if Osiris was joking.

Rourke jerked like he'd been hit. "You lie."

"Enough of this." Osiris gripped her closer and flashed them away.

Chapter Eighteen

As soon as Grace disappeared, Rourke followed. There was no time to discuss anything with Bishop or Creed. He found himself back in the woods where he'd met Grace.

The surprise on Osiris's face when Rourke appeared was gratifying, and he took advantage of it. He flashed again to behind them.

Rourke snaked his arms around his brother's neck and jerked him to the side. Grace staggered free as Osiris's hold loosened to wrestle Rourke.

An elbow bashed Rourke's ribs. He grunted in pain and kicked Osiris's feet out from under him. As his brother fell, he dragged Rourke down with him. They rolled through the grass. Fists flew. Rourke's mouth dripped blood. Osiris landed a knee in his gut. Rourke grunted as searing pain followed. An organ had to be ruptured.

"You've been such a fucking thorn in my side." Osiris's hands wrapped around his throat.

Rourke shoved his arms through Osiris's and forced them apart. Osiris's hold released.

Rourke drew his arm back and released a punch to his brother's nose. "Where's your demon now?"

Osiris flew back, alarm in his eyes, blood gushing from his nose. "I think he wants me to have it out with you. Get it out of my system. We've come to understand each other."

Diving to land on him, Rourke reached to snag his last stake. He pinned Osiris with a hand pressed to his shoulder, his knees in his brother's pelvis.

Osiris knocked the stake from Rourke's hand. Both rolled to dive for it, but Grace beat them to it. His brother's fangs bared, he bucked Rourke off, and lunged for Grace. With a roar, Rourke grabbed his legs and yanked Osiris back under him. Rourke held his hand out and on cue, Grace tossed the stake to him.

He snatched it out of the air, raised it high, and hesitated.

Had Osiris really tried to protect him? Rourke's memory was hazy, supposedly from one of the Circle trying to bond with him. Had Osiris suffered as much as he had?

"Do it." Black was bleeding into his eyes. Osiris shook from the effort of keeping the demon at bay. "He's taking over. He might look the other way when it comes to some things, but he won't let you win."

"I can save you." Rourke didn't know why he offered, other than he felt like he had to. They were brothers.

"The kid's in the basement. I couldn't hand any children over—not after failing you." His brother's bleak expression read defeat…and acceptance. "*Do. It.*"

Osiris knew he was beyond saving. If Rourke wanted to help him, to preserve anything of their familial bond—

Rourke slammed his weapon into his brother's chest just as the whites of his eyes disappeared. Osiris's eyes widened in agony, his mouth opened in a silent scream, his chest bowed out. Rourke jumped off of him. He swooped Grace up and put as much distance as he could between them and the yawning black chasm opening up under Osiris to drag his demon back to Hell.

Grace's heart clattered against his chest. Her arms wrapped around him and she buried her face in the crook of his neck. He glanced over his shoulder.

Ash fluttered in the breeze. The last of his family. His only regret was that Osiris's demon wasn't in his true form, that he was only sent back to the underworld instead of being dusted with his brother. He gently set Grace down.

She gazed up at him with watery brown eyes. "Are you all right?"

An emotion he didn't want to name plugged his throat. "We have to find the boy," he said roughly before flashing them back to the mansion.

***

As soon as Grace reoriented herself, she planted both of her hands against Rourke's chest. "Hold it right there, mister. I have something to say first."

Irritation shot through his expression. And too damn bad. She wasn't going to tiptoe around him until he decided to face his feelings and talk to her. Because *that* would never happen. Not with his emotionally sterile place and precise eating habits. He'd use the time to fortify the wall against her and spray it with repellent.

"We need to find the boy," he said with a growl.

"Call Bishop and Creed. I bet they've already found him." Her hands splayed across his impressive pecs, and she was in no hurry to move them, nor her gaze glued to his body.

"Grace—"

"Call them, Rourke. We were gone more than a few minutes. Those two wouldn't waste time looking for us."

He wore a scowl but made the call. "Did you find the boy?" He nodded and hung up. A dark brow arched toward her.

"You said your piece earlier. I need to say mine." She took a deep breath. "I'm sorry. I should've told you. But…you're *you*. You can handle yourself. The people who might be my parents, maybe can't. It's not like I gave him top secret information. I said you go out, investigate the killings, and that's it."

He opened his mouth to speak, and she laid a finger across his sensual lips. A predatory glint entered his dark eyes.

Her breath caught; her mouth suddenly gone dry. "I fed from Ophelia with no problems."

Rourke drew back as if the news disturbed him. Yeah, it bothered her, too.

"But," she continued before he made any more excuses for why he should avoid her, "I still love you." He went rigid. "Bonding ability or not, I want an us. At least give us a chance."

She dropped her hands from him and waited, a jumble of nerves.

His shoulders slumped, his gaze dropped, his voice was low. "I don't deserve you, Grace. You have your whole life in front of you with your prime family. Don't waste your love on me."

Ah, that word—prime. It explained everything behind Rourke's motivation in life.

"Ozias Rourke. You have a thick skull." She cupped his face and dragged it down to hers. "I can't think of anyone else I'd rather shower with my love. And shower with."

A low rumble in his chest preceded his lips crashing down on hers.

Yesss. Nothing was crystal clear, or written in stone, but he'd basically given her a passcode to his mental barrier. She'd take it.

He opened his mouth for her. The smoky flavor she'd missed so much filtered onto her taste buds as her tongue tangled with his. Her hands drifted down to spread across his body, resting on his muscular shoulders.

His arms wrapped around her. If his guns weren't poking her in the stomach, she'd probably feel his massive erection pressed into her. Gradually, he pulled back. A deep maroon of desire tinted his dark brown irises.

That was so hot.

"I want you in my bed, Grace." His expression was more serious than a declaration of *I want to fuck you.*

She blinked, trying to determine the meaning behind his words.

"My bed…" He paused, uncertainty in his expression.

"I've never been in your bed," she blurted out. That was it. He was saying something significant and it had to do with the mysterious piece of furniture that had stolen him from her side after they'd been intimate.

He inclined his head in agreement. "I had slept," his features hardened into the terrifying vampire slave who'd killed his masters, "in filth, on the floor, for well over a decade. Then I slept in alleyways, still in filth. After I teamed up with Demetrius, we were intent on taking down our former government that I slept wherever required.

Once the compound was built, I made damn sure I bought a top of the line mattress."

A warm smile curved her lips. "And Betty keeps you stocked in pristine sheets."

He scowled. "And pie. I fucking love her pie. I want to tear into it with my bare hands."

She realized the admission he'd just made. He wasn't speaking figuratively. She'd seen his restraint over meals.

"One night a week, we can have an eat-with-your-hands meal."

Alarm passed through his expression. "Why would I want to do that?"

She sighed and caressed his cheek. His bonding instinct might be the least broken thing about her male. "So you know you aren't that helpless kid anymore, that it's your choice."

His muscles shivered under her skin. Her words had gotten to him.

He laid his forehead against hers; he had to hunch significantly to do it. "I don't deserve you."

"We deserve each other. We deserve to be happy. If we can't bond when we say the bonding vow, then we'll make our own ritual."

"Grace," he whispered. He lifted his head, his thumb stroked her lower lip. Such a little movement earned maximum physical response. "Before I take you, I want you to feed from me. When you kissed me, I had a hard time getting past Ophelia's taste on your lips."

A chuckle bubbled past her lips.

It earned her another frown. "I'm not kidding. For a second, it was disturbingly like kissing a…"

She understood why he didn't finish. The guy just dusted his only living relative. "Sister. It's okay, Rourke. Ophelia and the others are your family more than Osiris was."

At the name of his brother, his gaze dropped. "I think he was actually telling the truth. At least in his mind, he was trying to protect me."

"It's messed up, but Osiris did seem to have a thing about not hurting kids." Adults, obviously, were a different story. "I think your home environment left a huge opening for corruption, but he drew a line and stuck to it. My memory of him was him wandering around the house I was in. He should've easily sensed where I was. And Ari—"

"Is here." Bishop's voice boomed across the lawn. He carried a little boy with thick black hair and brown eyes as wide as saucers.

Creed exited the mansion with a tiny blonde in her mid-twenties clinging to his arm. Her wild curls framed her face like a fluffy halo, and her sky blue eyes stared at Creed like he was every Hollywood heartthrob from the twenty-first century.

Her scent was a surprise. Human.

When they got closer, Creed tried to pry her arm off him. It didn't work. "She was the boy's nanny. Osiris abducted her to watch him and feed him."

Grace gasped and faced the girl. "Did you know about…us…before that?" How terrifying would that have been for the woman?

She shook her head, her riotous curls flying. "I was leaving work, and he snatched me out of the mall parking lot, like *poof*. And then I was here, and vampires, and a kid *with fangs*." Ari giggled and held his arms out to her. He was enough to persuade her to disengage from Creed. She hefted the boy from Bishop and planted him on her hip. "I mean, vampires? But Ari's so sweet, and that man told me what happened." She choked on the words and hugged Ari tightly. "Dear child. What will happen to him now?"

Grace warmed to her instantly. The woman asked about Ari's future, as if the fate of her own life paled in comparison. Was that what her own parents had been like?

"We'll take care of him," Bishop said with confidence.

Grace glanced at Rourke. He wore a troubled expression as his gaze flicked back and forth between Bishop and the child.

Was it because Ari wasn't prime or because the compound wasn't a place to raise a kid? Or both? Grace was sure that was it. Rourke and his team couldn't raise Ari, not with their violent lifestyle, and he feared no other family would step up.

She stepped in closer to him and discreetly laid a hand on his back in reassurance. He slanted her a searing look, and just like that she wasn't worried about him anymore. Thankfully no one noticed because the human hadn't quit talking.

"It had to have been awful what happened to him," she said in a hushed voice, oblivious to the sensitivity of vampire hearing, that Ari would hear every word. "I lost my parents when I was a kid, too. It just messes with you, you know? And that!" Creed flinched. The girl shook her finger. "That's why that hot guy kidnapped me. No trail, he said. It'll be easy to dispose of you, Melody, he said. God he was cruel. Hey!" Her finger aimed toward Rourke. "You look like him."

The poor thing paled and inched closer to Creed. The normally easygoing vampire watched her out of the corner of his eye, unsure what to do with her.

"He was my brother, and he won't harm you any longer." It was the gentlest Grace had ever heard Rourke speak. Her respect swelled for her mate at his show of consideration.

"Is he a good guy?" She clutched Ari close and leaned into Creed, who took a step back from her.

"Yeah," Creed said, like *duh*.

"Oh, okay." She shot Rourke an apologetic look. "Then I'm sorry."

All of them watched her, wondering if she was for real.

Rourke recovered first. "Flash her and Ari back. Demetrius will sort out what to do."

Bishop and Creed disappeared with Ari and the woman who was still talking.

"At least the landing will finally shut her up," Rourke said.

Grace chuckled. "Nathaniel spewed all over my shoes the one time I flashed him, but I thought it was because we'd been drinking."

"I think…" He faced her and ran a lock of her hair through his fingers. "I think I may love you, Grace."

That might not be enough for many females, but it meant the world to her. "Then I think I'll stick around until you know for sure."

A slow, sexy smile spread across his handsome face. "Didn't I mention my bed earlier?"

***

Rourke stood next to his mate in front of the closed door to Demetrius's office.

"What if they don't like me?" Grace had faced her worst nightmare. Bedded him even. But meeting her parents for the first time in twenty-three years shredded her.

"You know they'll love you." Rourke's calm tone seemed to upset her. "You've had a whole day to adjust to knowing they're your parents. They've had a whole day to adjust to knowing their daughter is still alive. It's time."

Grace gulped and faced the closed door. "Can you come in with me?"

He dropped a kiss on the top of her head. "No, angel. You have my full support, but your parents deserve you. You deserve to have time alone with them."

"They're your family, too, now."

He cocked an eyebrow. He admitted he'd come a long way in the short time he'd known Grace. She had spent the entire day in his bed. And much of the night until Demetrius summoned them for the meet and greet. It was a huge change in Rourke's world, but he wasn't going to go declaring a prime couple Mom and Dad.

"They'll love you as much as I do." He yanked her in for a quick kiss on the lips. Then he spun her around, opened the door, and tenderly pushed her inside. He swept the door closed behind her.

He released a long breath. It'd be a lie if he said he wasn't worried Grace's reunion with her parents meant she'd want to go live with them and make up for the decades they'd lost.

"You're very good with her," Betty said behind him.

He spun slowly, not wishing to let the ancient vampire know she'd snuck up on him. Although it made sense one as old as she should know how to.

Betty trudged up to him and raised her wrinkled hand to pat him on the shoulder. "And she's very good with you."

Hyped up on the surge of emotion his mate caused within him, he rested his hand on top of hers. "Betty, I love your pies."

The smile materializing on her maternal face cracked another fissure in his hardened soul. "Ozias

Rourke, wait until you try my apple crisp. There's one cooling by your door."

Hellfire, he might have to let out his pistol belt a couple of notches. But…maybe he could wait for Grace at his place. Wait, *their* place.

He thanked Betty and turned to go when the office door opened.

"Rourke." Grace's voice was flushed with happiness, her eyes glassy from joyful tears. "Come in and meet my parents."

Pivoting, he met Grace's excited gaze. Behind her stood the couple from the picture, wearing welcoming smiles.

Rourke's heavy past rolled off his shoulders. His future stood in front of him.

Epilogue

Rancor's fangs dripped yellow pus. "You discovered *nothing*?"

He sat on the dais, surrounded by bones. New ones had been added since Fyra's last visit.

She swallowed nervously, going so far as angling her head to expose one breast under her fiery red locks. Any distraction at the moment only behooved her. "He's proven stronger than expected. I need more time."

And it wouldn't do any good. That frustrating blond Adonis clung to his *loyalty*. She mentally snorted. *As if.* In the underworld, loyalty was worse than timidity.

What was Bishop's issue anyway? His priority should be her! He'd fed from her, said the vow. She should *rule him*.

Rancor rose to his full, terrifying eight-foot height. He stalked down the wide steps, his curved horns throwing off glints of the torches lining the walls.

Show no weakness. Fyra took a step back. Bollocks. Where was Stryke to throw under the bus when she needed him?

The distance between them was eaten up until he loomed over her, the chamber's constant stench of terror and death smothered her. She took another step back. The side of his mouth curled, revealing even more square footage of his fangs.

Tusks were more accurate.

"Rancor." Curses, her voice trembled. "I can fix this."

His voice dropped to a husky drone. "You'll make something right." He fisted her hair and used his claw on the other hand to slice it off until her breasts were fully exposed.

Oh shit, oh shit. It was going to happen. Her mama told her it was inevitable. *You're smarter than them, Fyra. Do* whatever *it takes to stay out from under them.*

Mama. No! Fyra couldn't show any more weakness with Rancor inches away.

"Now, now, Your Greatness. I have a duty to attend to." She attempted to skirt around him toward the archway that led to an ice cavern. She knew it like the lines on Bishop's face. When her heat overwhelmed her, she sought solace in the cavern.

Rancor grabbed her shoulders, his claws digging in. She bit back a cry.

She tried one more avenue. "Didn't I hear Stryke got his ass sent back from the human world within minutes?" He was a strong male—and not Rancor's type, usually. Stryke was her go-to distractor.

"He's being dealt with."

His claw stoked down her torso, cutting skin along its path. Her loincloth was ripped off.

Fyra darted to the left. He caught her and dragged her back against him.

He bested her in size and strength, proving immune to her coercion, if only she could flash like the vampires.

Vampires. Her link to Bishop. Was it strong enough? Of course not, he resisted her, but she had to try.

She closed her eyes and summoned his image. Pretending it was the same as entering the hosts Terrance recruited for her, she allowed the same ethereal sense of vaporizing her physical body to take over.

The rough flesh of his fingers stroked the underswells of her breasts. His hot, fetid breath choked her. She squeezed her eyes shut harder. Bishop. Think of her bond with the big lug.

Fresh air assailed her.

Her eyes flew open. No, she wasn't outdoors. She was in the bedroom Terrance performed his summons in.

It worked. Fyra sucked in a breath of relief.

Dread wiped out the relief. She was an underworld fugitive. Going back was not an option. Second tier now meant nothing. If she went back, she'd be on the menu, the next pile of bones on the dais—and grateful because what she would go through before would be, well, Hell.

She straightened. Fear could suck it. She escaped Rancor; she was bad ass.

A tingle of awareness spread along her spine. Her bond to Bishop was strong enough to transport her here and fuck the middle man. That meant he could find her. And he kinda hated her.

Plans clicked into place. Rancor would dominate the next prime sucker to fall for the Circle's bullshit so he could hunt her the fuck down and finish what he'd started. She would become the Circle's bitch before they ate her alive. Then regurgitated her to gobble her down again.

She needed clothing, a hat to hide her distinct hair, and money because that's what fueled this world.

***

The sun would rise in a few hours, but Bishop was stretched across his bed, seeking refuge in his apartment per his new nightly routine when he wasn't working.

She'd been quiet.

Bishop wouldn't say he missed his demon's voice. He didn't. Really.

But where was she? What was she planning? When would she turn up again?

His body reacted to the last question. *No, you idiot. Think about something else.*

The events of the night. Yes, those. How nice it worked out that Grace's parents took in Ari.

Grace's little brother and Ari played and fought like natural brothers. The chatterbox, Melody, even went with them as a live-in nanny. She had endeared herself to the family as quickly as she had to everyone else. Except for Creed.

Bishop laughed to himself. He loved seeing his brother-in-arms uncomfortable and Melody certainly did that to him.

A hot flash blew across Bishop's brow. His head swiveled around, searching for a reason. Another flush of heat lit him up from the inside out.

She was here. On Earth. His demon was in town.

Why did he feel it now?

He scrambled his brains for a reason, and it was obvious. With Terrance dead, she had no host. But she had Bishop and their bond. His demon was walking in this realm in her true form.

He raced outside, avoiding everyone lest he have to answer any questions.

He scented nothing. No brimstone, no being roamed the trees surrounding the compound. Where would she be?

The house where he'd seen the blonde host she'd used before. It was his only lead.

He crashed back inside to load up on gear and weapons. He'd find his demon and make her pay.

Thank you for reading. I'd love to know what you thought. Please consider leaving a review at the retailor the book was purchased from.
~Marie

About the Author

Marie Johnston lives in the upper-Midwest with her husband, four kids, and an old cat. Deciding to trade in her lab coat for a laptop, she's writing down all the tales she's been making up in her head for years. An avid reader of paranormal romance, these are the stories hanging out and waiting to be told between the demands of work, home, and the endless chauffeuring that comes with children.

mariejohnstonwriter.com

Facebook: Marie Johnston Writer

Twitter @mjohnstonwriter

Also by Marie Johnston

The Sigma Menace:
Fever Claim (Book 1)
Primal Claim (Book 2)
True Claim (Book 3)
Reclaim (Book 3.5)
Lawful Claim (Book 4)
Pure Claim (Book 5)

New Vampire Disorder:
Demetrius (Book 1)
Rourke (Book 2)

Pale Moonlight:
Birthright (Book 1)
Ancient Ties (Book 2)

Bishop
Book Three, New Vampire Disorder
To be released April 2017

When had Bishop Laurent's life become a barrel of secrets? It all started with his birth, but he's moved beyond his circumstance to become one of few vampires trusted by their government to protect and serve their people. Until a demoness tricks him into bonding with her, intending to use him as her own personal informant. Loyalty remains paramount and Bishop resists her attempts to gather information on his team.

Unfortunately, Bishop's knowledge was the only thing protecting Fyra in her realm. On the run from the entire underworld and an angry Bishop, she uses all her wiles to keep her freedom. Only, Bishop is just as crafty, hunting her down, and turning the tables. Now she's his prisoner and her influence over their bond holds no sway on the determined male.

To escape the demons sent to hunt her, it'll take working together and delving into Bishop's past to get them out of the mess the demoness landed them in.

Printed in Poland
by Amazon Fulfillment
Poland Sp. z o.o., Wrocław

60137080R00168